Alanna stood still, listened. There was the mumble of voices, the slap of feet on hard wooden floors. Then she heard it. Childish voices singing.

She turned down a side corridor, following the sound, and came to a door—the door of the nursery. She opened it a crack.

There were a dozen or so children sitting on the floor, gazing up at a young woman who was reading to them. Alanna couldn't quite work out what was happening. The children had to sing or cheer or shout when certain words came up. Whatever it was, they seemed to be enjoying it.

She looked from child to child, opened the door a crack more. There, on the right of the teacher was…her daughter.

Eleanor was wearing a little blue frock, she had dark hair, she was smiling. Alanna felt her heart beat as it had never beaten before. She stood there, completely unable to speak.

Her daughter. So beautiful.

Dear Reader

2008—Mills & Boon is a hundred years old. A big birthday, a time to look back, to reflect on past successes.

When my first book was accepted I was invited to Richmond for lunch. I was nervous, excited, I knocked over the bottle of red wine. My editor gave me an amiable and knowing smile. Obviously I wasn't the only first-time writer she had taken out to lunch.

My first book—COUNTRY DOCTORS—was sold to Mills & Boon in 1996. So this is my twelfth anniversary. I have now written forty-two books, and am looking forward eagerly to the award I will be given to celebrate my fiftieth. Mills & Boon have translated and published my books in eleven different languages. It's a weird thrill, seeing your story in Hungarian or Swedish.

Mills & Boon really feels like a family. I regularly meet editors and other writers for drinks, lunch, at a party or a conference. We phone each other constantly. If I'm stuck, if I've got an apparently insoluble problem, then help is always available. If I'm phoning, e-mailing, or dropping in and demanding a coffee—I know I'll be welcome!

Writers of even longer standing tell me it's always been like this, so here's to the next hundred years!

Gill Sanderson

THEIR MIRACLE CHILD

BY
GILL SANDERSON

MILLS & BOON®
Pure reading pleasure™

First published in Great Britain 2007
Large Print edition 2008
Harlequin Mills & Boon Limited,
Eton House, 18-24 Paradise Road,
Richmond, Surrey TW9 1SR

© Gill Sanderson 2007

ISBN: 978 0 263 19965 9

Set in Times Roman 16¾ on 20 pt.
17-0708-53809

Printed and bound in Great Britain
by Antony Rowe Ltd, Chippenham, Wiltshire

Gill Sanderson, aka Roger Sanderson, started writing as a husband-and-wife team. At first Gill created the storyline, characters and background, asking Roger to help with the actual writing. But her job became more and more time-consuming and he took over all of the work. He loves it!

Roger has written many Medical™ Romance books for Harlequin Mills & Boon. Ideas come from three of his children—Helen is a midwife, Adam a health visitor, Mark a consultant oncologist. Weekdays are for work; weekends find Roger walking in the Lake District or Wales.

Recent titles by the same author:

A BABY OF THEIR OWN
THE DOCTOR'S BABY SURPRISE
A SURGEON, A MIDWIFE: A FAMILY
A NURSE WORTH WAITING FOR

CHAPTER ONE

Now Alanna Ward knew that this was a mistake.

She had put off the day she intended to arrive and had then been unable to sleep the night before. She had stayed the night at a friendly bed and breakfast hotel in a village some distance from Benthwaite. Then she had told the landlady that as she wanted to set off early, she wouldn't need any breakfast.

And she had set off early, very early. In fact, even though it was summer, it was still dark as she slipped out of the door. The landlady had left her a packet of sandwiches, which was kind.

Alanna was used to early morning walking. In some of the places she had lived, it was the coolest time of the day and she had always loved the dawn. But now the dawn didn't bring her any great joy. She was making a mistake.

She could have waited and taken the bus. Instead, she'd decided to walk the ten miles to her destination, following a path over the Lakeland fells that she remembered well. She was in no hurry to arrive. She was not even sure what she was going to do when she arrived. Or, for that matter, why she was doing it.

Still, it was a wonderful walk. It was early summer, the air was fresh with the smell of dew-damp grass and there seemed to be a clarity in the air that had not been there in the city. Right, she was enjoying herself. She was moving, on her way to something new. This had been her life for so long.

On her back was the rucksack that held much of what she owned. Certainly all that she needed. She had wandered, swapping continents with little more than the contents of that rucksack. And she guessed that, perhaps after a couple of bitter-sweet days in Benthwaite, she'd be wandering again. If she was moving, then she was content.

She intended to enjoy the walk. But then she topped a steep incline and found herself slightly out of breath. She knew what she was doing. She was pushing herself harder than was necessary. Trying to avoid thinking. Trying to avoid remembering. But she couldn't help it.

This was the country she had grown up in, the route one she had followed so many times. Usually with her childhood sweetheart, Finn Cavendish. She smiled sadly to herself. She had never loved anyone as she had loved Finn then.

Both sets of their parents were dead, and they had been brought up by single elderly relations, who had done what they could but hadn't really known how to cope with young people. It hadn't been their relations' fault, Finn's uncle, her aunt. Both had tried to show love, but had not succeeded too well. Now both were now dead.

Alanna and Finn had been thrown together. After months of caution they had relaxed their guard little by little and then had learned to delight in each other. It had seemed like something that would last for ever. It hadn't. She had been ecstatic when she had married him. And yet, two years later, they had parted. The gulf between them had grown too great. She didn't exactly hate him, but she hated what he had done to her. And perhaps what she had done to him.

So now, four years after parting, perhaps it was time to get things sorted out. She had never bothered to get divorced—vaguely she wondered if Finn had divorced her. Could he do it without her knowing? She wasn't sure. If so, it wasn't entirely his fault. As she left she had deliberately cut off all contacts, never writing to old friends, never leaving a forwarding address as she'd flitted from nursing job to nursing job, across Africa, South America, even Australia and New Zealand.

She reached the highest point of the walk, a narrow defile between two peaks. There was a shudder of remembrance as she sat on a rock, unslung her rucksack and pulled the damp shirt away from her back. She wiped her face with the red and white spotted bandana tied round her neck. She had been moving faster than she'd realised.

Below her, two miles way, was Benthwaite.

From up here it looked like a fairy-tale little town. There was its river running into a lake, green fields surrounding the grey stone buildings. And in the distance the ever-present brooding grey fells. She had been born there. Had grown up there, been happy there. She had attended its little primary school, sung in the choir of St Mary's church. She could see its spire. It was odd, though. In spite of her love for the place she had always known that she had to wander. The cause of her problems?

She drank from her water bottle, reached for her packet of sandwiches. Memories were flooding back and with them came the certainty that this was a mistake. Why once, in this very spot, behind that rock, she and Finn had nearly…

There was a blush on her sun-bronzed cheeks. He had stopped them going too far, not her. He was older, had had to be wiser. But it had seemed so right to them. They'd never spoken of it then but they'd both known that in time…

So what was she doing here now? All right, she had a few days to spare. She was in England for three months. She'd had a job offer in Peru, which sounded good. Quite often she had worked for a charity called SAMS—South American Medical Services—which had established a series of clinics all over the continent and was always looking for—cheap—medical staff. When she'd returned to England the head of SAMS had asked her to come and talk to him.

Gabriel Buchanan, sometimes known to his staff as the Angel Gabriel because of his golden hair. And because he was always certain that he was right. He was an odd mixture of hard work, charm and ruthlessness. He got things done.

'This is the job you've been looking for,' he had told her. 'This is promotion. A complete new complex, high in the mountains. I want you to be matron of the medical wing. The job is settled, there'll be plenty of funds, a bit of luxury even. Alanna, I know and you know that you're the right person for this job.'

Well, it had sounded good. As ever, Gabriel had sold it to her as if there could be no doubt in her mind.

'But I don't want to settle down yet, Gabriel.'

'You do, though you won't admit it to yourself. I can see it in your eyes. You've been running long enough, now's the time to put down roots. Among people who need you and will come to love you.'

She smiled at the memory of his enthusiasm. Gabriel could be forceful—but she was not easily pushed. Probably she would go to this new complex. Perhaps this time she would not move on, as she always had done before. Perhaps somewhere there was a place that would content her, quell her constant urge to see what was over the horizon.

Anyway, she had told Gabriel she would let him know. Forget the future, live for a while in the present.

She finished the last of her water and sandwiches, leaned back against the rock and looked round her. More memories came crowding back. She had seen mountains on three continents. Most of which would dwarf England's Lake District. But these mountains still had a hypnotic power, a beauty that meant that she could be happy here. Could she?

She had wandered as if looking for something

but never had really found it. Because she didn't know what she was looking for. Just for a moment she recalled her favourite childhood film, *The Wizard of Oz*. (Though the wicked witch of the north had frightened her.) Dorothy's famous line—'East, west, home's best.' Well she was home now. But it didn't seem best.

She was being stupid! She stood, heaved the heavy rucksack onto her back. She was here to settle things. She would see Finn. Time should have healed all pain as well as letting love drift away. But for a moment she stood, undecided. She could still turn back, walk away, disappear again. As she had done before. But then she looked round the well-loved scene and decided not to. What was that word? Closure? She wanted closure. She wanted things settled. She started the two-mile trek down to Benthwaite. Perhaps this could all be over by the next day and she could take the bus out—to wherever.

The village—little town really—didn't seem to have changed. It was strange, seeing it after so many years. There was a tightness in her throat as she approached and once again she wondered if she ought to turn round, leave this place for ever. Any business she had with Finn she could presumably manage by post. She had intended to book into another bed and breakfast, wander around and make a few enquiries during the day and then go to see Finn tomorrow morning. Why was it necessary to see him?

She turned a corner and there was St Mary's church. An attractive building, built in the local grey stone, she had always liked it. Casually, she glanced at the nearest lichen-covered gravestone. Edward Makins, 1871-1959. Eighty-eight, not a bad lifespan.

For a moment she thought of another scene, high in the desolate Yorkshire moors with the rain rattling against their anoraks. She and Finn had poured the ashes out of a tiny urn into the rushing waters of a stream. Then they had looked at each other, but neither had been able to find anything to say. There had been nothing to say to each other. Perhaps it had all started then, perhaps that had been the beginning of their end. She didn't know. She felt the tears well, but wouldn't let them go. She had to be in control.

She turned, swiftly walked away. She had come here to see Finn. She wanted to be cool, detached…not unfriendly but certainly not intimate. And this place was having an effect on her.

She walked onwards. Now she was passing the cottage hospital—Rosewood, it was called. Here she had done her first little bit of voluntary work, here she had decided to be a nurse. Eventually.

It was a handsome building, a converted old hall with a couple of more modern wings built on behind. There was a front lawn and gardens, carefully kept. And a line of trees along the road edge to shield the noise of passing traffic. She slowed, stayed half behind a tree and looked.

A Land Rover drew up outside the building, a man climbed out, walked round to the other side of the car. She recognised him at once, there was no mistaking that walk, the contrast between the leanness of the body and the broadness of the shoulders. Finn, Finn Cavendish.

Well, she had come here to see him. But it was still a shock to have him there in person.

She realised that he had become a distant memory but now he was a real person again. She slipped further behind the shade of a tree. He mustn't see her.

He came back from the other side of the car—and he was holding the hand of a little girl. Finn picked her up, whirled her round and the little girl was obviously delighted. Then, very clearly, Alanna heard her speak. 'Daddy, Daddy, are we going riding tonight?'

Alanna reeled with the shock. Daddy? For some reason she had never considered that he might have remarried. And now he had a little girl—about three or four? Not far off the age that their daughter would have been…not far off the age that… And then she heard his voice. It had been half-forgotten, but there was that deep husky tone that had always thrilled her.

'Yes. We'll go riding, Eleanor. I've phoned Jane, she'll be waiting for us and she'll have a saddle on Daisy.' And then they were gone together through the front door.

Alanna slumped against the wall. Eleanor. He had called the girl Eleanor. They had talked for hours about naming their child, it had been a happy distraction for them both. She remembered lying against him, one hand holding his hand, the other on the swell of her belly, feeling the kicking inside. Finally they had decided to pick one of three names. Anna, or Louise, or Helen. Couldn't he have called this child something different from Eleanor? So close to one of the names they had picked together for their... dead...child.

It was the beginning of the summer season, things were getting busier at Rosewood Cottage Hospital. Inside the crèche, Eleanor was still holding Finn's hand and managing to jump up and down. He knew what she was pretending to be. 'I'm a bouncy horse, I'm a bouncy horse. Daddy, we're going to Jane's tonight so I can ride on Daisy? She said we can go any time.'

Finn sighed. It wasn't what he really wanted. It was not a good idea, he had thought that he might visit Jane a little less often. But he couldn't resist his daughter. 'We'll go and you can ride on Daisy,' he said. 'Jane will be pleased to see us both.'

In fact, he knew that, although Jane was obviously pleased to see Eleanor, it was him that she really wanted to see. In a dozen subtle ways she had made it obvious that she'd like to know him better. And it was obvious that they were well suited. They liked each other. She was divorced, he was…well, he didn't know what he was. Certainly alone. But he had to make it obvious to her that he wasn't interested in any long-term relationship. And he knew she wouldn't settle for less. He wasn't interested in marriage. He'd been there, done that. And bore the scars. Tonight he'd have to find some gentle way of telling her that they had no future but friendship. He felt sorry—but that was the way it was.

He let go of Eleanor's hand at the door of the crèche, gave her her lunchbox and kissed her. Then he watched her run with a scream of joy, to join her friends and Lucy, who ran the nursery. She was a happy little girl. And he loved her more than he could say.

* * *

Finn leaned against a white-painted fence, watching his daughter solemnly riding a Shetland pony around the edge of the paddock. This was the first time she had ridden on her own without Jane, the riding-school owner, holding Daisy's bridle. Eleanor obviously felt the importance of the occasion.

'She's coming on,' said Jane. 'She loves it but she's not too confident. That's good. You know, if she keeps this up, she'll want a pony of her own in time.'

'If she wants a pony, and when you think she's mature enough to look after one, then she shall have one. Keep it here?'

'It's the best stable for miles,' Jane said cheerfully.

'Why be modest when you've got nothing to be modest about?' Finn turned to Jane and winked as Jane laughed.

She was a very attractive woman, he thought. Perhaps a couple of years older than him. Her face was vivacious rather than beautiful, people paid more attention to her when she spoke than when she remained silent. Tight riding breeches and a white shirt showed that riding was good exercise, she had the lithe body of a much younger woman. A man who had Jane as a partner would be very lucky…

Finn felt half-content. The early evening sun was warm on his back, he'd had a good day at the hospital. He lived in a beautiful part of the world and his daughter was happy. What more could a man want? Well, he supposed there were some things. And there were some things he had to do that rather saddened him.

Jane put her hand on his arm, a small gesture of affection. 'I love seeing young people on horses,' she said. 'They seem to…to understand each other.'

'I know what you mean.'

As they stood side by side in easy companionship he wondered again why he couldn't think of marrying her. There was so much going for them. Then he realised. Once he had been in love. Really, truly in love. It had ended in pain. But still he could remember that almost breathless feeling of wanting to do nothing but be with his lover. Be with Alanna. And he couldn't feel that magic with Jane now.

'I had a letter from my ex-husband this morning,' Jane said, perhaps too casually. 'He's moving to New Zealand and doesn't think he'll come back. So he's out of my life for ever.'

'It's good to make a clean break,' Finn said after some reflection. 'I've never told you, but I'm still married. I haven't seen my wife for over four years, haven't heard from her either. But I still feel married.'

'I see,' Jane said, and smiled at him sadly.

He realised that she had got his message.

That night, after the bath and the necessary story, when Eleanor was fast asleep, he went into his storeroom and took out an old photograph album. Then he poured himself a small whisky and sat to leaf through the album. There weren't many pictures. Alanna had always been in too much of a hurry to stand around and wait for photographs to be taken. Even the pictures taken outside the registry office where they had been married were hurried. And there was one picture that summed up all there was to be known about Alanna. She was standing on a mountaintop, hands on her hips, long hair ruffled by the wind. The smile on her face showed it all. She was confident. She could take the world by storm.

He wondered if she had.

They had been opposites—perhaps that had been part of the attraction when they'd been younger. She had been the wild one. He had been the conventional one, hard-working, career fixated.

He was different now. He had changed, had discovered there was much more to life than work. Here in Benthwaite he was more than the local doctor—he was one of the community. He knew the names and histories of most of his patients. People stopped him in the streets, asked when would be a good time to come to see him. They also often asked for an instant diagnosis, well, that was the down side. He had joined in the church quiz team. He was a member of a local climbing club, even a member of the mountain rescue team. His life was happily full. He was a contented man—almost.

He stared at the picture of Alanna, wondered where she was. What was he going to tell Eleanor about her? He winced. It would be dreadful.

CHAPTER TWO

IT WAS work as usual at the cottage hospital next morning. He sat by the pregnant Emma Pearson's bed and stole a couple of her grapes. 'Emma, you're right. It's going to be hard managing without one of our practise nurses. Especially you. But somehow we'll manage.'

'But I want to work! I'll not do all my hours, just a few, and—'

'Emma! How many times have you told people that they are not to get out of bed until they're thoroughly fit? That they're not to do "just a few hours?" That they start work again when the nurse—that's you—or the doctor—that's me—tells them that it's safe to do so?'

'Well, quite a lot, I suppose,' grumbled Emma. 'But it's different when it's yourself.'

'No, it's not. Look, you've had one miscarriage. You've been seen by Charlie Rankin, who's the best obs and gynie consultant for miles. He thinks you'll be all right this time—he's sutured your cervix with a Shirodkhar stitch. All you have to do is take things easy. Now, you do want this baby, don't you?'

'There's nothing I want more!' Emma's voice rose. The she sighed and said, 'That's what I like about you. You're always right. Ever thought how irritating that can be?'

'All the time. Now, listen. You work in this place. You know better than anybody what needs doing. You are not—I repeat not—to get out of bed and try doing it. Okay?'

'OK, Finn. I'll be good.'

Finn stooped and kissed her on the cheek. 'I'll be in every day with the gossip,' he said.

He'd finished his rounds at the hospital, now he had a couple of house calls to make. It was another beautiful day, he was looking forward to a short trip out into the country. As he walked out of the ward, Stella, the hospital matron, came out of her room to speak to him. 'Message from Harry. Can you ring him at once? Before you set off into the countryside, he says. Come into my office and do it.'

As was customary, all mobile phones had to be switched off in the hospital.

Harry seemed a little uncomfortable on the phone. 'I don't know whether this is good news or bad news,' he said. 'I had a caller this morning. Only afterwards did I find out that she wasn't from the Agency; she was asking about the temporary replacement for Emma. But she's a very well-qualified nurse and at the moment unemployed, so I think she'd be good for the job. But if you don't like her for any reason, then that's fine.'

'Harry, I've every confidence in your ability to pick a nurse. What does Ross think?'

Ross McCain was the other partner in the practice.

'Ross is happy with her but he again thinks you should have the last word. It's your decision. If you don't like her for any reason then we don't employ her and we're happy with it. You understand that?'

Finn was surprised. It was unusual for Harry

to feel he had to spell out things so clearly. 'I understand,' he said.

'Fine. In fact, the woman hasn't made her mind up yet. Perhaps she won't like working with you.' Harry's voice was ironic.

'Always a possibility. When do I see her?'

'She's in the committee room right now. Can you come straight over?'

'I'll be there in ten minutes.' This seemed like a bit of luck. He had just told Emma that they could manage without her. But he knew it would be hard. To get an experienced practice nurse just like that—they were lucky.

He was at the practice in less than ten minutes. The receptionist told him that the young lady was waiting in the committee room and Harry had said he was to go straight in. She'd send in coffee in a few minutes, once they'd had time to introduce themselves. All seemed fine. Without a care in the world Finn ambled upstairs to the tiny room they called the committee room.

He opened the door, walked in. He noticed fresh flowers on the coffee-table, the pile of magazines in the corner. The room was lit by a large window. Sunlight was pouring through it and the applicant sat in the shadow so he could barely make her out.

The woman stood, stepped forward. 'Hello, Finn,' she said. 'It's been quite a while.'

Finn stared at her, open-mouthed. It was Alanna.

There was a rush of emotion so wild that he didn't know what to make of it. He didn't know if he was angry, happy or bewildered. But, whatever it was, the feeling was so intense that for a moment all he could do was stand there and stare. It was Alanna. His wife. Yes, as far as he knew, she was still his wife. And somehow she had drifted back into his life. This was a shock he could have done without.

Somehow he managed to mutter the most pointless thing of all. 'Harry should have said it was you.'

'I asked him not to. I wanted—I needed to see you see first. I suppose it's a bit of a surprise.'

'It's a lot more than a surprise,' he said.

He looked at her more carefully now. And he was aware that she was studying him. He hadn't seen her for four years and she'd, changed. Well, he supposed he had changed too. Her outfit was typical Alanna—jeans and a T-shirt. She had never seen a need to dress up. Her long hair was now short, and slightly bleached by the sun. Perhaps she was a bit thinner—though she had never been fat. But her body was still as feminine, as curved as ever.

Her face was different—it, too, was thinner. But her old expression was gone. There was no wildness in her eyes. She looked calmer or more weary, he didn't know which. Perhaps it was both. And then it hit him like a thunderbolt. She was still as gorgeous as ever.

This was the woman he had loved. Once. And the thought of that made him angry.

What should he do now? Kiss her hello? Just sit and look at her? He remembered the bitter words when they had parted. Alanna saying that she just couldn't stay with him, he saying that he didn't want a woman whose reaction to trouble was to run instead of fight. Still, that had been four years ago. Should he try to kiss her?

She solved his little problem by offering him

her hand to shake. The first physical contact for four years, her grip was firm and she didn't, as he had expected, let go of his hand at once. 'You're obviously surprised to see me,' she said.

'Surprised? Shocked would be a better word. Alanna, what are you doing here? I hear nothing from you for four years and then you just wander in.'

She nodded. 'I suppose it was a bit inconsiderate. But I didn't want to get in touch with you first in case afterwards I didn't have the nerve to face you.'

'Right. Understandable, I guess.'

They stood opposite each other in silence. There was a knock at the door and a girl entered, carrying a tray with cups and a pot. It was Millie, their latest young employee in the office. She glanced curiously at the two silent figures and said, 'I brought the coffee.'

'Thanks, Millie. Just leave it on the table.'

Putting the tray on the table seemed to take longer than it should have, and when Millie finally departed Finn said, 'Well, we might as well sit down.' So they sat and stared at each other.

Alanna had had longer to prepare herself for this meeting so she started the conversation. 'You're looking well, Finn. Country life obviously suits you. You're not as thin as you used to be, and you're looking tougher. Not working so hard?'

So, he thought, this was to be a conversation as it might be between two old casual acquaintances, not estranged husband and wife. 'I'm working hard enough. But I prefer life here, it's more personal. I get to know people, they aren't just cases that pass through my examination room. And I love the area. I've always loved the mountains.'

'I've been around a lot of mountains myself,' she said.

'Quite. Which particular mountains?'

She shrugged. 'I started in Africa where I did a lot of famine relief work. Then moved over to South America after a year and travelled quite a bit there. A lot of work at high altitude.'

He nodded. 'I tried to get in touch. Letters were returned, saying no one had heard of you.'

She felt slightly guilty about that. 'I changed my name. From Cavendish to Ward. You won't remember, it was my mother's maiden name. I didn't want to be found. I thought the break should be clean.'

'It was certainly that.'

She shrugged. 'I just didn't feel married any more. And anyway I'd given you your ring back.'

'So you had. Thrown it at me, to be exact.'

'Bitter words, bitter times Finn. That was four years ago.'

'And how did you find out that I was here?'

She shrugged again. 'It was no great problem. There were people at our old hospital who remembered you very well, remembered me, too. They told me you had moved here.'

Finn was still trying to make sense of things when something struck him. 'Just a minute! Harry brought me here to interview a temporary practice nurse! That can't be you?'

'Why not? I'm qualified to do the job and it's work that I'm good at and enjoy. Don't forget, like you, I grew up here. Harry thought I might fit in. And it'll only be for a few weeks.'

'But what about…? What about…?'

'About us?' she asked.

'About us. Don't think that it won't hurt. It will, it'll hurt both of us.'

She had thought of that already, had worked it through. 'It'll hurt all right, and I know that people will talk. But there's something that we need to get sorted. Our marital status. It'll be easier if we can do it together.'

'Of course,' he said. 'I think I need some coffee.'

Alanna realised that they both needed time to think. She had prepared herself for this, had nerved herself to meet him. But it was still harder than she had expected. Seeing him brought back so many conflicting memories. The happiness. And the grinding misery.

He poured her some coffee, then poured himself some. Black, just half a teaspoon of sugar. And he didn't just stir it once but a dozen times, round and round and round. It was an unconscious little habit he had always had, she remembered it so well. It was the little things that hurt. It reminded her of the happy times when…

Yes, this was harder than she had thought it would be. She had intended to be calm, cool, to discuss things dispassionately. And her coolness was rapidly disappearing. She drank her coffee in silence, then said, 'So you gave up the idea of being a big city consultant and came back home? No more losing yourself in work, determined to be the youngest A and E consultant ever?'

She hadn't intended her voice to be brittle, hostile even. But that was the way it had come out. He didn't take offence, but she remembered that once he would have.

'Yes, I gave up the big city. I think I do as much good here as I did there. Besides, there's more to life than work. What about you? Have you enjoyed what you've been doing?'

She thought a moment before answering. 'A lot of it has been hard. I turned out to be like you…like the you you used to be. I lost myself in work. In fact, we seem to have changed characters. You seem much calmer, not so desperate to get on. And I'm working so hard that I'm as bad as…' Her voice faltered. 'As you used to be.'

'I remember. How many jobs have you had?'

'Two countries in Africa. Famine relief work, it was…hard. Then I moved to South America and wandered around there a bit. In between I had a few months in New Zealand and Australia.'

'Always the wanderer,' he said.

She felt the unspoken challenge, had to respond to it. 'You seem to have adapted to life without me quite quickly,' she said. 'Yesterday I was outside the cottage hospital when you drove in. I saw you by accident.' In spite of herself, her voice quavered. 'You had a little girl with you, she called you Daddy. And she was lovely. It upset me so much that I turned round and was going to walk out of Benthwaite again. But then I decided I had to see you at least once—whether you were married or just living with some woman.'

Now she felt stronger, the anger was taking over from the hurt. 'I can't blame you for looking for happiness with another woman. I can't blame you for having a child. But did you have to call her Eleanor? So close to one of the names we picked for our child? You were the father, I was the mother! You remember, our dead child?'

She didn't get the reaction she had expected. She looked at him in amazement as he leapt to his feet, his coffee-cup dropping from his hand. She thought that even when going through those evil months of constant argument she had never seen him look so distraught. 'Oh, God,' he said, his voice anguished, 'it was the shock of seeing you. I'd forgotten. How could I?'

She stood, too, almost frightened by him. He seized her, took her shoulders in his hands. She felt an odd sort of thrill in his touch—she couldn't work out what, it wasn't sexual. But it felt good to be held. She gazed into his tormented face. Just what was wrong with him? So he'd had a child, named her Eleanor. Perhaps it was really no big deal. Whatever it was, she could see he had problems with it.

'I told you I tried to get in touch,' he said. 'I tried hard, I really did.'

He looked down at the spilt coffee then for a moment occupied himself with wiping the tabletop with tissues. He poured himself some more coffee, in silence offered her the jug. She pushed her cup towards it, he refilled it. She could see that he was trying to get his thoughts in order, she'd seen him do that before. Well, she'd give him time.

She had to get her own thoughts in order. She guessed that his attempts to find her had something to do with a divorce. Perhaps he wanted to marry the mother of the little girl. Well, that wasn't her problem. And, besides, she was here now. He could have a divorce if he wanted. And then she would be on her way. But for some reason she felt sad.

Eventually he spoke. 'What did you say to Harry when he offered you this job?'

She shrugged. 'Don't forget that me and Harry go back a long time. So for that matter, do you and Harry. He encouraged us both to take up medical careers. But when I called he thought at first that I was from some temp agency. In fact, I was just looking for you.'

'And after a few minutes chat he offered you a job?'

'He said he'd have to check with his two partners. I said I'd think about it.'

'Did he say anything about me and you?'

She shook her head. 'I thought he was going to but he didn't. He said whatever I had to say to you was between you and me. But, of course, he knows about us separating.'

'Of course,' said Finn. 'Next question. Why do you want to come and work so close to me?'

'I'm not sure. I was thinking about that just now. I suppose I wanted closure. I was going to offer to divorce you if you wanted. Get things between us finally, officially sorted out.'

'And then wander off again after a few weeks?'

'I suppose so. I've got a very good job offer in Peru to start in three months. It's work I'd be good at—and it's got better conditions than most. But I'm only thinking about it.'

'I see.'

She saw him lift the telephone on the table, ask the receptionist to get Harry to phone him the moment he was free. Then he sat and looked at her. She had no idea at all what he was thinking. This was all very different from what she had expected.

The phone rang—it was Harry. Now Finn was in control again. She remembered how calm he could be at the most tense moments. It had been a valuable quality in an A and E doctor. He never got excited. Good for the doctor. But how it had angered her when they had argued.

Unashamedly, she listened to Finn's side of the telephone conversation. 'This new nurse, Harry, came as a real shock. You might have warned me… Perhaps you're right, it was a shock that I needed… I'm…coping… Harry, can you take my afternoon surgery? I've finished at the hospital, I've a couple of house calls to make. I thought I might take Alanna with me…. Yes, I know she's not a member of the team yet, not insured…. I'll just take her for the ride… Harry, one last thing. You're certain you're happy about this job offer? OK, I can veto it. I'll give you my decision this afternoon.' He rang off.

Alanna thought that now Finn was more in control. But not completely. There was some-thing worrying him. But she knew better than to ask him, it would all come out in time. She said, 'You'd stop me working with you, Finn? That's a bit vindictive, isn't it? I know me working here might hurt you. But it's going to hurt me, too.'

He looked at her and to her slight dismay she thought she saw another feeling that she hadn't expected. Pity? Him feeling sorry for her? He ought to be more worried about himself.

'I've got a couple of calls to make,' he told her. 'I'd like you to come with me, it'll remind you what this kind of medicine is like. Call it a working interview.'

She looked down at her jeans and T-shirt. 'Not dressed like this,' she said. 'I need a uniform. Can I borrow one?'

'No problem.' He phoned Reception, asked them to find a nurse's uniform—he even remembered her size. Two minutes later the uniform was brought in by the even more curious Millie. And a fitted-out nurse's bag. 'You can change in the room down the corridor,' he said. 'We'll make my two calls and then we'll have a talk.'

'You don't think that we've said everything that has to be said?'

'No.'

'So a talk to iron out a few problems?'

He shook his head. 'You just don't know,' he said.

* * *

He took her out to his Land Rover—a vastly different car from the sleek Jaguar he had owned in Leeds. This one was, well…not exactly battered but it had obviously been in some rough places. She tossed her rucksack into the back of it and instantly felt at home.

They left Benthwaite, drove along little roads and then turned onto a small track. Her heart lifted as she looked around her. This was—well, this had once been—her country. She felt alive here. Not a lot was said as they travelled. She glanced at him from time to time and saw that he was feeling the same as her—simple contentment at being there.

After a while she felt she just couldn't help herself. 'There's Gentle's Crag!' she exclaimed. 'Remember when we got to the top and—'

'I remember,' he said curtly, so she didn't say any more. Sometimes it wasn't a good idea to recall past joys.

They bounced onto a smaller track, glad of the four-wheel-drive. 'We're going to see Jake Thomas,' he told her. 'He has a farm up here, works it with just himself, his wife and one farmhand. He had an accident with some farm machinery, got a really bad slash across the abdomen. Lost a lot of blood. I moved him to the cottage hospital in time, got plasma into him and then sutured the wound. We kept him in for a while and then sent him home to convalesce. I keep an eye on him.'

Don't tell me,' she said. 'He doesn't like just lying around while there's work to be done.'

'Got it in one. But if I drop round every now and again, I think I can hold him back.'

She thought for a while. 'You didn't send him on to Carlisle? The big hospital there?'

'We have to send serious cases there. But the A and E department at Rosewood is pretty good for the smaller stuff. There's a couple of good nurses who can handle most of what turns up and I'm often ready to turn out for anything a bit more complicated.'

'I thought cottage hospital A and E departments were being run down?'

'They are and it's madness. We provide a great service for the locals. We can cope with most injuries, and when the visitors come we get really busy. It would be almost impossible to ship them all off to Carlisle. There has to be some kind of intermediate station between the GP and A and E in a large hospital. And we're it.'

'You used to say that everyone should go to a large hospital A and E when you were a registrar in one.'

'I did. And I've changed my mind.'

Without thinking, she told him, 'I've worked in a lot of small hospitals. I know what a big difference a little bit of skill and a lot of dedication can do.'

'Quite,' he said, and she decided he didn't want to hear too much about her experiences abroad.

After a while he said, 'So we're just going to look in on Jake and I'd like you to change his dressings.'

'Checking on my professional competence, Doctor?' she asked with a little grin.

'Not at all, Nurse. You were always better at dressings than me. I remember.'

But remembering was the last thing either of them wanted to do at the moment so neither of them said anything more.

He drove into the farmyard. She remembered

the sight, the smell, felt happy. He led her to the open farmhouse door, shouted inside and then took her into the stone-floored kitchen. He smiled at the farmer's wife, who was standing by the sink. 'Hi, Betty. How's he been?'

'Like the way he's been all his life. Awkward. But I can cope. Cup of tea?'

'Love one. This is Nurse…Nurse Ward, by the way. She's working with me today.'

'Two cups of tea, then. I'll have them ready when you come out.'

Finn took Alanna into a room opening off the kitchen. There, lying dressed on the bed, was Jake, He had once looked tough. Now she saw his face was pale and drawn and his eyes red-rimmed.

Finn's voice was friendly, joking, not the voice of a doctor talking to a patient. 'You're a lucky man, Jake. I've brought a nice nurse to visit you. This is Alanna Ward. Now, tell me how you've been. Taking it easy, like I told you?'

'Good to see you Dr Cav. I'm all right, things are mending.'

'You've not been moving around too much?

Just into the kitchen and the yard? And then only to look?'

Alanna saw Jake's eyes shift guiltily. 'Well, it's hard sitting here, doing nothing, all the time. Perhaps I might have—'

'Jake! If that cut opens you'll be in hospital for weeks! Now let's have a look. Nurse, can you…?'

Jake leaned back on the bed, undid his shirt. Alanna took gloves and scissors out of the nurse's bag and carefully cut away the dressing. Then she stood back for Finn to look at the wound and went into the kitchen to ask Mrs Thomas for a bowl of warm water. When she returned Finn and Jake were having a casual conversation about the price of sheep. This was not the intense A and E registrar that she remembered.

He smiled at her, stood back so that she could clean the cut and skin around it, then re-dress it.

'That was a nasty cut,' Finn said over her head. 'So you're still in pain. Pills not working?'

'I don't like taking pills. I'm taking the antibiotics, like you said, but I can stand a little pain. I don't want to get addicted and—'

'The pain keeps you awake at night?'

'Yes but—'

'Jake! There's no chance of you getting addicted! Painkillers are there to help you. You'll get better quicker if you take them and get a good night's sleep. OK?'

'Right, Doc,' muttered an embarrassed Jake.

'Keep that up and I'll be in to see you some time next week. You've done well so far. Don't spoil it.'

A quick word with Betty, a cup of tea each and then they were bumping down the track again.

'It's a common problem among older men,' he muttered, 'especially around here. They think there's something masculine about suffering pain.'

'I've come across it,' she said.

While they had worked together she had felt an ease between them. She had worked for him in A and E in Leeds, and they had been a good team. They could anticipate each other's needs, and for a couple of moments that feeling had returned. But now they were distant again.

She glanced at him, saw him frowning. Something was bothering him but she was not going to ask what. He might tell her.

Their next call was at a village about five miles

from Benthwaite. They drew up outside a little cottage at the end of a terrace. The front garden had obviously once been loved but now it was neglected. There were weeds in the flower-beds, the lawn desperately needed cutting.

As they stepped out of the car they heard a knocking—Alanna saw that it was coming from the window of the cottage next door. There was an arm beckoning them. 'Where are we going?' she asked.

'The patient is Mrs Malvern, she lives in the cottage and she's eighty-five. The lady knocking from next door is Mrs Trent. She's a good neighbour, we'd better go and see what she has to say. In fact, it was she who phoned the surgery.'

They went in to see Mrs Trent. They were shown into a tiny spotless living room, smelling of expensive polish and with every possible surface sparkling. There were family photographs in neat rows. Alanna had glimpsed the kitchen—a much more friendly room, with a TV muttering on a shelf.

Alanna recalled what Harry had called this kind of room. He'd called it a God room. Lots of older people round here had them, were very proud of them. They were for guests and for Sundays. They weren't for everyday use.

Finn introduced her and Alanna said, 'This is a lovely room, Mrs Trent.' And she meant it.

It was the right thing to say. Mrs Trent liked the praise. 'I like to keep things nice,' she said, blushing slightly. 'Dr Cavendish, you've come to see Mrs Malvern?'

'I have indeed. I gather that you phoned the surgery asking us to look in. Very neighbourly of you.'

Mrs Trent blushed again. 'You know I keep an eye on her—drop in every morning, help her to bed at night?'

'Yes I do. She's very lucky to have you next door.'

Mrs Trent shrugged. 'Nothing to it. We've been neighbours for thirty years and when I had two kids at home I couldn't have coped without her. She was an angel to me. So the little I can do now I'm happy to. But I'm afraid that after that fall she had, she's got worse.'

Finn sighed. 'I thought she might. Breaking

your femur at that age—lots of old people used to die after it. Now we've got antibiotics, they usually survive. But they're rarely the same as they were. Is there anything new, Mrs Trent?'

Mrs Trent looked sad. 'I've had a call from our Jennifer in Birmingham—you know, she's having another little one in a month? Well, things have got a bit tense for her—so she asks if I can go down and look after Glen and Peter till after the baby's born. I've got to go, Dr Cavendish. But that leaves Mrs Malvern on her own and she can't... I want to help her but Jennifer's my daughter and...'

'There's no problem Mrs Trent. You go to Birmingham and look after your grandchildren. I'll make arrangements about Mrs Malvern. I'll phone Social Services and see that she gets the best of care. There'll be someone round either this afternoon or tomorrow morning.'

'Mrs Trent beamed with relief. 'Thank you, Doctor. I want to do what I can but...'

'You're a wonderful neighbour. I wish all my patients had someone like you next door.'

Alanna saw Mrs Trent smile with pride at that.

This was a new Finn to her. What had happened to the intense man she had married? This Finn was different.

They went next door and, as instructed by Mrs Trent, just walked in and shouted. There was evidence of someone having done some cleaning—probably Mrs Trent, Alanna thought—but there was also a smell that she recognised at once. The very opposite of the smell in Mrs Trent's house. This was the smell of old people and neglect.

Mrs Malvern came out of her kitchen, walked slowly towards them. 'Dr Cavendish—how lovely to see you.'

'Lovely to see you, too, Mrs Malvern. May I introduce Nurse Ward?'

A polite handshake, a trembling hand. Alanna could feel the thinness of the skin, the bones so near the surface. They were shown into another God room—but one not so well kept.

'How have you been, Mrs Malvern?' Finn asked gently.

Mrs Malvern had to consider this question a while. 'Well, I'm getting a bit forgetful but it's always good to see you. I don't get about as much as I used to.'

'I hear you've had a fall,' said Alanna. 'It must be hard washing yourself. Would you like me to help you?'

Another pause for reflection then Mrs Malvern said, 'That would be very nice of you, dear.'

Alanna looked at Finn who nodded. 'Take as long as is necessary,' he said quietly. 'You're the nurse.'

Alanna helped the old lady to her bathroom, undressed her and then saw her safely in the bath. Leaving the door open, she went to the bedroom—and sighed as she saw the mess. But she found some clean clothes. Fifteen minutes later she took a much spruced-up Mrs Malvern down to where Finn was waiting. Apparently very patiently. Finn patient?

'I'll make Mrs Malvern some tea while you chat,' she said. 'How do you like it, Mrs Malvern?'

'Yes, dear,' was the answer. So Alanna went to make tea as best she could and through the open door could hear Finn asking questions. 'Who is the Prime Minister, Mrs Malvern? Can you add thirteen and four? What happened in 1945?' Alanna sighed. These were the questions designed to discover just how bad Mrs's Malvern's condition was. And she wasn't doing very well.

Fifteen minutes later they drove away from the cottage. 'What are you going to do about her?' Alanna asked.

He shook his head. 'It's a common story. There's not enough work around here for young people so they leave. Houses are bought by rich incomers so couples can't afford their own homes. People like Mrs Trent and Mrs Malvern—their families have to move away. Mrs Malvern has one daughter, but she moved to Australia with her husband.'

'So what's the answer?'

'We work closely with Social Services. I get on with them well. I'll arrange for the district nurse to call round regularly. And I think we'll try to get Mrs Malvern moved into Cadell House. It's a nursing home, we keep an eye on the patients and it's got a good staff. She won't like leaving her cottage, but these decisions have to be made.'

'You like this sort of work, don't you?' she asked after a while.

'Very much. I like to see all sections of the community—from birth to death. And I like keeping in touch.'

'You've changed. You used to like the quick turnover in A and E.'

He thought about that. 'I did. But then I dealt with cases, not people. Now there's more… wholeness in my work and I like it.'

'I see,' she said thoughtfully. 'Have we any more cases?'

And it was a while before he answered. Then one taut monosyllable. 'No.'

'So do we spend the rest of the afternoon together?'

Another monosyllable. 'Yes.' Then he added, 'We have to talk.'

She realised that the two calls they'd made had been more than just part of his job—they had been a means of keeping his mind off something that he thought important. 'Finn, if it's so hard for you, I can just walk away. Leave you for your wife or mistress or whatever and your daughter. Most things between us are now gone.'

He couldn't keep the harshness out of his voice. 'You can't just walk away,' he said. 'You just can't. Alanna, you might not think it but this has been easy for you so far. And now it's going to be one of the hardest days of your life.'

'But how…? What…?'

'Just wait and see,' he said.

Alanna thought that she was tough. In the past few years she had been in some hard situations, had needed all the nerve she'd had to get herself out. But now something in his voice sent a chill through her that she had never felt before.

CHAPTER THREE

THEY drew up at the side of a stone house on the outskirts of Benthwaite and she fell in love with it at once. It looked sturdy but welcoming. At the front was a neat orderly lawn and she could see through to the back where there was a large conservatory and a play area for children—a plastic slide and swing. A lived-in house.

Is this yours?' she asked, rather coldly. She remembered the flat they'd had in Leeds. It had been large, comfortable, but basically just somewhere to live. It hadn't been a home. Of course, they'd had plans about a home eventually, somewhere out of the town centre. But the plans had come to nothing.

'This is mine. I like it here.'

'Will your wife be in—or the person you are

living with? Do you want me to meet her? What will she say when I turn up?'

'I have a cleaning lady but no wife. To be exact, unless you've divorced me in some outlandish place or other, the only wife I have is you.'

It was a weird feeling to hear him say that. She was his wife. She said shortly, 'I haven't divorced you. But what about the little girl?'

'I…I'll tell you about the little girl. In time. Let's just go inside now. We'll eat first and then we'll talk. I've got some soup and I'll make you a sandwich.'

'Fine,' she said. She knew that something was coming up. But she would let him tell it in his own time.

He took her to his living room and she fell in love with that, too. It wasn't a God room, it was a room to be lived in. There was a large fireplace at one end, a couple of comfortable squashy leather couches, a thick red carpet that echoed the pastel colour of the walls. There were books, CDs and toys here and there.

She could hear him rattling around in the kitchen. He'd never been this domesticated when they'd been married. Most of the time they had either eaten out, had something delivered or bought ready-made meals. He had changed.

But she couldn't settle. There were three pictures of Eleanor on the wall—she was indeed a lovely child. And that made Alanna angry. She decided that she had made a mistake. She was not going to stay here as a nurse. She would tell him at once.

He came in carrying a tray, set it down on the coffee-table. She said, 'I've just made up my mind. I'm not going to stay here. We'll decide about the divorce right now and then I'll be out of your life at once and for good.'

There was a long pause and then he said, 'Eat first and then we'll talk. You can make any decision then. And I'm afraid things are a bit more complicated than you realise.'

There was that look again. Half assessing, half pitying. She didn't like it, she felt that it meant bad news. But what possible bad news could there be?

The vegetable soup was home-made, thick, and tasted far better than anything out of a tin. He told her the sandwiches were made with local cheese and tomatoes. It was a simple meal but it tasted like a feast.

They ate in silence, and then he took away the dishes and returned with two glasses and a bottle of whisky. She looked at him in amazement. 'Finn! You never drink in the middle of the day. And I certainly don't.'

He poured them both a small measure. 'Today is different,' he said. 'Think of it as medicine. You know we've both been avoiding talking since you came into the surgery this morning. Talking seriously, that is. Well, now we have to talk. No matter how painful it might be—to either of us.'

There was an edge to his voice that Alanna hadn't heard before. It shook slightly, as if he was hurt. Hurt? Finn? The man who was always in control?

'Why did you come back, Alanna? What's in it for you?'

It was a harsh question and it angered her. 'Closure,' she said. 'We're unfinished business, we might as well get things wrapped up neatly. We were in love, we got married, we were having…having a baby. The baby died and I suppose our love died, too. End of story. You drove me away, now let's have a neat finish.'

'I drove you away! What rubbish is that?'

She was still angry. 'You might not have intended to, but you did drive me away. Whatever we had had together, it went. I needed support from you and I got none. You retreated inside yourself, you were unreachable. I knew you were hurting—well, I thought you were hurting. But you wouldn't admit it. Everything I tried to do for you, it was no good, I couldn't get through. And when I needed comfort, you told me we had to get over it. Get over it! Was that comfort? Finn, I had lost my child!'

Now there was a definite tremor in his voice. 'Let's be exact, Alanna. We lost our child. I had feelings, too.'

'Then why didn't you show them?'

'I tried,' he said. 'I really tried.'

'Perhaps you should have tried harder! I loved you, Finn, and I reached out to you for help but you weren't there. You should have been the one steady place in my life and you were gone.

You had been the only man I had ever loved and I felt I was living with a stranger. So I left you. I had to, nothing I said or did could touch you. I still hurt when I think about what I went through. In fact, I'm hurting now.' She paused to take a breath. 'It was leave or go mad. I felt that things would never be right again.'

'I felt I was a stranger. I felt you were, too. And I was ...sad when you left.'

'Sad? You were sad?' It didn't seem much. But by now her anger had evaporated. 'I loved you,' she said sadly, 'right to the moment that I left, I loved you. And I think you loved me. But it went and now it's time to draw a line under things.'

She saw he was thinking, puzzled, trying to work out what to say next. Eventually he said, 'I'm afraid we can't draw a line. Things have... changed.'

By now she was definitely uneasy. She reached for the glass, took a sip. 'Let's have it,' she said. 'I know there's been something more hanging over you—over us both—ever since I came back. So what is it?'

She saw he was trying to relax in the chair

opposite her and not really succeeding; he too sipped his whisky.

'I'll ask you one thing,' he said. 'Hear me through to the end. We need to go over some things that may be painful, get them in order. And then we'll…we'll see. OK?'

'Right,' she said, feeling more uneasy than ever.

'And remember, I've been through all this already. And I know what it's like. So try to…to hold on.'

Hold on? A feeling of horror crept over her. 'What do I need to hold on for? I've been through everything already haven't I?'

'Not entirely,' he said.

'We were having a baby. I wasn't sure at first, a lot of men aren't, but as your belly swelled and I could feel the baby kick against me when I was next to you in bed, I was the happiest man alive. I had you. And I was getting another little you.' He stopped, looked at her.

He shouldn't do this to me, Alanna thought, it's hurting. The past was the past and they both knew where it was leading. But she would be silent a little longer.

He went on, 'Then things went wrong. You were eight months pregnant. You'd done all the right things—exercises, classes, check-ups, diet. We'd bought stuff for the baby, it was a text-book-correct pregnancy.'

'Very textbook!' she said bitterly. 'And look what happened.'

'Please! Keep calm, Alanna!'

Even in her distress she found she rather liked the way he said her name.

'You were eight months pregnant, everything was going well and I was away at a conference in Scotland. Only a phone call away. It was January, there was a storm and it hit all of the British Isles. You had gone to visit a friend you knew from your wandering days in Africa. A small mill town some forty miles away.'

'That storm was nearly as bad as some of the storms I've seen in Patagonia,' she murmured.

'It was certainly bad. You left your friend, were on your own, were walking to the railway station when you slipped and cracked your head against a wall. A serious skull injury. Picked up by ambulance and taken to the nearest hospital.

It was a small hospital, nothing like the major place where we both worked. And that night A and E was overcrowded and short-staffed. The place was bedlam.'

'I know all of this already, Finn. Why do we have to go over it all again? It's too painful.'

'I know it's painful, but you tell me what happened next. You need to relive it.'

'But I told you, I don't want to relive it!'

'I know you don't. Please, Alanna, trust me. There is a point to this.'

So she relived that fateful time. 'In hospital they found out that not only did I have a suspected fractured skull but also that the baby was coming. In fact, my skull wasn't fractured but I was concussed. So I was sent to the maternity unit, and fortunately there was only one other patient there. Only one other mother-to-be. It was fortunate because the maternity unit was the most understaffed in the hospital. And the midwife they had was young and inexperienced.'

She had to stop, remembering the pain, the desperation. 'And all I wanted was you. Where were you? I needed my husband with me. I know they tried to get in touch with you, but…'

She could see his face was haggard, realised he was suffering as she was.

'The hospital got in touch with me. I was desperate but there was no way could I move. Railways, roads, both blocked. You'd have to have the baby on your own. And you were only half-conscious because of the concussion.'

'I don't remember much of the birth,' she said. 'I remember feeling love for…for my child, and feeling sad that you weren't there but it didn't matter too much. You were coming. It seemed to be a straightforward birth. At first.'

'It was. You had your—our—baby. A little girl. You kissed her and held her to your breast. And the midwife decided that she was a month premature, perhaps, just for the night, she ought to go to the special care baby unit just as a precaution, and you were happy with that. Just about that time the other woman had her baby and she was sent to SCBU as well, just as a precaution. It was all a mad rush and for a while nurses had to be borrowed from other departments.'

'Get on to the next bit,' she said, knowing that her voice was agitated. 'Get it over with quickly.'

Even in her distress she could tell that he was as hurt by this as she was. So why did he have to continue?

'Next morning you were told that your baby had died. No cause, no reason, it just happened. SIDS. Sudden infant death syndrome. Rare, but it happens. You were taken to SCBU and there was a tiny form. Your baby. Dead.'

'That's as much as I want to hear!' She leaped from her seat. 'I'm going, this minute! Do you think I don't remember every evil moment of that stay? Finn, I've never forgotten so why are you making me go through it again? You were never deliberately cruel to me—why start now?'

'I never forgot either! We were both hurt, remember? Now, sit down, just sit down and just listen. We need to go through with this as it happened.'

She sat after a moment. She reached for the glass of whisky and needed two hands to hold it.

His voice shaking, he went on, 'So that was our baby dead. And we both coped in different ways—or didn't cope. I lost myself in work, you pined after the freedom you had felt while travelling. And we argued non-stop. Ten months later we parted. Apparently for good.'

'We did,' she said, defiant. 'I waited till I was certain that I wasn't suffering from baby blues, and then I went. I felt I had to.'

Then of all thing he came over to sit by her and took her hand. She wrenched it from him. 'I don't want you to touch me,' she said. 'Whatever I feel, I can cope with it on my own. I've done it for long enough.'

He shook his head. 'This isn't like anything before,' he said. 'And I'm trying to help.' But he went back to his own seat. He went on, 'Two years after our baby's death, months after you had gone, disappeared apparently off the face of the earth, I got a phone call from the maternity consultant at the hospital where you had your baby. It was urgent that I come to see him at once. So I went—though I was reluctant to. He told me that a woman had just died in the hospital. She'd had rapid-onset cancer. But in the examinations that had taken place before she died, it was discovered that she had a genetic abnormality. Her children would be in danger of developing adult polycystic kidney disease. So obviously her children had to be tested. In fact, she only had one child.'

'This is very interesting, but what has it to do with me?'

'Rather a lot. The woman who died was the woman who had her baby at the same time as you. Her baby went into SCBU at the same time as yours.'

Alanna saw him force himself to lean back in his chair, to try to relax. His voice was calm but there was a tension in it that seemed to communicate itself to her. 'Listen carefully, Alanna. The dead woman was a single parent, a bit of a loner, her child was being looked after by Social Services. So it was easy to test the child to see if she had inherited the genetic abnormality. She hadn't inherited it but the genes showed that there was no way that the mother and child could be related.'

Alanna had difficulty in taking this in. 'Not be related? That makes no sense.'

'The hospital staff were mystified, too. But they searched through hospital records and eventually, reluctantly came to the obvious conclusion. The dead woman's baby and our baby were born at the same time, taken to SCBU at the same time by an inexperienced midwife to an overstretched department. The babies were swapped round.'

Alanna blinked and thought. It was just possible. In a stressed ward, with an inexperienced midwife and two new babies who, let's face it, had looked very similar. It was very unlikely but it was just possible. Yes, possible.

Almost conversationally she said, 'That means that it wasn't our baby that died. It was hers. My baby lived.'

'Your baby is alive, she's a lovely little girl. She lives with me. It's Eleanor.'

It took time but the full enormity of what he had just told her suddenly hit her. It made the whole of the past five years meaningless. Her baby was alive—but she had buried her, mourned her, slowly come to live with her death. It had all been pointless.

Again she leapt to her feet, the glass of whisky crashing on the coffee-table. Her hands reached for her head, grasped it as if to contain the realisation that her life had turned suddenly, irrevocably upside down. Desperately she turned to the photographs of Eleanor on the wall. Yes, that was her daughter. Now she looked closely she could see herself, in the bone structure round the eyes, in the curve of the lips. What was she to do? How could she cope? She screamed—louder than she had ever screamed in her life. And then there was merciful blackness.

When she came to she was lying on the couch, Finn looking down at her, holding her hands. She felt him gently push a strand of her hair from her forehead. She was only half-conscious and thought it had been a dream. He was looking at her the way he used to look at her. Then what he had told her came hurtling back.

'My baby's alive?'

'There's no doubt about it. She's ours. Half you, half me.'

She's nearly five and I've never known her.'

Alanna rolled over to face the back of the couch, her body racked with sobs that seemed to come from the depths of her soul. She didn't know what to think or feel. Everything she knew, everything she had built her life on was a lie.

She felt Finn's arm around her, holding her lightly. She turned towards him, grabbed him and pulled him to her. Her arms wrapped around him, she leaned against his chest, felt the strength of his arms holding her. And slowly the sobbing stopped. She lay there silent, glad that he didn't yet want to talk. Then she eased him from her, sat upright. She knew she must look a mess, she didn't care. There were so many questions to ask, so much to decide.

Finn was looking at her. She could see the understanding in his eyes. 'If it's any comfort to you,' he said, 'when I found out I wept, too.'

She looked down at her shattered glass on the coffee-table, the whisky pooling around it. He guessed what she was thinking, passed her his own glass. 'Just sip,' he said. 'It'll help a little.'

She did as he suggested and the fiery liquid gave her strength. 'Why didn't you tell me?' she asked. 'Why didn't you find me and tell me? I would have come.'

'I tried to find you. No one could have tried harder than I did. I even employed a private detective. But you'd deliberately tried to lose yourself.'

'I want to see my daughter,' she said.

'Of course you do. But there are things we have to talk over first.'

I don't want to talk! I want to see my daughter!' She knew her voice was becoming shrill, there was nothing she could do about it.

He leaned towards her, took her by the shoulders and shook her. 'Alanna! You've got to be strong! We both have got to be strong. This is not about you and me—there's a third person now and she's the most important. She's already had a hard time. Taken from the only mother she ever knew when she wasn't quite two. You can't just rush to her, say that you're her mother— what do you think she'd feel? You've got to think of her welfare!'

'I *am* her mother! Whatever happens!'

'You are. No one will deny it. But you've got

to take things slowly. She's a person now, Alanna, capable of making up her own mind about things. You can't just parachute into her life saying you're her mother. You've got to take things slowly!'

She had difficulty taking this in. Did he not feel as she felt? He claimed that he did. 'Finn! You're being the cool, collected doctor again! You've got to think before you feel, plan everything ahead. It's the bit about you that I used to dislike…or, at least, not understand. How can you stand back and—'

'Alanna! You're being selfish again! Just like old times. You're thinking that your feelings are all that matters and that…' He paused and she saw him force himself to relax. 'We're arguing again,' he said. 'And there's no need. It fact, it isn't possible. Alanna, we're both responsible for this little life. We both have to work together to make her happy.'

There was silence for a moment. She lifted the whisky to her lips, then put the glass down again. She needed to keep her mind clear. She suspected that she was going to make some of the most important decisions of her life over the next few minutes.

Calmly she asked, 'Could I have a mug of tea, please?'

'I think that would be a good idea. I'd like one myself.'

She went on, 'I must look a mess. Could I go to your bathroom first for a while?'

'Of course. There's one in the hall.'

'Then we can have a talk. And I promise not to get…to get emotional again.'

'You're entitled to get emotional.'

He took her to the downstairs cloakroom, found her fresh towels and suggested that she might even like to have a shower.

'I think that's a good idea. Will you fetch my rucksack from the car?'

'Of course. At once. Now, take your time.'

He fetched her rucksack, tapped on the bathroom door to say it was just outside and then went back to the living room. He picked up his whisky glass, raised it to his lips then, like Alanna, put it down again. He, too, needed a clear head. He fetched a brush and dustpan and a damp cloth, and cleaned up where Alanna had dropped her glass.

Then he waited for her. The past half-hour had been as painful for him as it had for Alanna. Though he could remember how painful it had been for him when he'd discovered Eleanor was alive. But now there were two people involved. Eleanor and Alanna. He had to get his own feelings in order. His own wishes.

He had genuinely tried hard to find Alanna. But when at first he hadn't succeeded he'd slowly come to the feeling that she might never return. Eleanor was his, and his alone. He had been happy with that.

He wondered why Harry had offered her a job, hadn't warned him that Alanna was coming back into his life. Then he decided Harry had been wise. Harry had known them since both of them had been children, knew about Eleanor's apparent death and about their subsequent break-up.

He would have been able to guess Alanna's state of mind if he had told her about Eleanor. Better for him to face that.

Then he started to think about himself rather than Alanna. He had recognised a side of the old Alanna in the last couple of minutes of their conversation. The Alanna who had gone so quietly for a shower was a much more dangerous creature than the distraught woman who had just learned about the existence of her daughter. She could be capable of anything if she felt strongly about it. And he doubted she'd ever feel more strongly than she did at the moment.

He had been so happy the last two years with Eleanor. He hadn't felt the need to share her with a partner—he had been engrossed in his child. Of course, Alanna was entitled to feel just the same as him. She was entitled to be the mother to her child, and he knew that she'd be a good mother. But where did that leave him?

Was Alanna still a wanderer? Would she want to take Eleanor away with her? Of one thing he was certain—she wouldn't be parted from her daughter, not for long. If necessary, she would fight like a wildcat for her young.

There was another thing that he hadn't really considered yet. What were his feelings for

Alanna now? For Alanna as a woman, an ex-wife, not Alanna as a mother to Eleanor? There had been that instant attraction that the passing of time hadn't changed. But they'd been married. It hasn't worked.

She was as gorgeous as ever—in fact, more so. The tiny touch of extra body fat had gone, her face had settled, grown thinner, her cheek-bones become more defined. The bubbly attraction of youth had changed to the deeper beauty of maturity.

What was the future? No, the question was, what was *their* future? Would Eleanor bring them together or tear them even further apart? Leaving him more heart-broken than ever. Eleanor was now his life.

He thought of himself as an honest man, tried to be as honest with himself as with anyone else. So he had to recognise the truth. For four years he had tried to put Alanna out of his mind but now she had returned. And he had to admit it to himself. The feelings he had for her had been buried deep. But they were still there.

CHAPTER FOUR

SHE came back from the shower and he could tell just by looking at her that she was a different person from the one who had gone in. She was still wearing the nurse's uniform but its severe lines seemed to emphasise the authority in her face. Now she was her own woman.

Her damp hair was brushed, her face made up. No sign now of the distraught woman who had felt she looked a mess. But it wasn't just that. There was a set to her shoulders, a confidence in her walk. Emotionally, she had been shattered—but she had recovered. Certainly the emotions were still there but they were under control. They would give strength to what she had to say. He managed to smile at her, but inwardly he shivered.

She sat opposite him, looked at where the broken glass had been. 'Sorry about breaking your glass and sorry that you had to clean up after me,' she said. 'I was a little upset. But now I'm fine.'

She took the mug of tea that he had made for her, drank from it and calmly asked, 'When do I see my daughter?'

My daughter. There was a clear assertion of rights. But it wasn't the time to fight yet. She was entitled to this first meeting and he knew how unsettling it would be.

'She's in the crèche in the cottage hospital. I usually pick her up when I've finished my day's work. It's an open-ended kind of arrangement that works very well. I don't want to disturb her routine. We'll fetch her at five and—'

'Finn, I've not seen my daughter for four years. I didn't know I had one until ten minutes ago, There's a lot of catching up to do and I...'

Finn was not happy with this. 'You need distance for a while,' he said. 'I know it has been hard so far and it's going to get even harder. You can't expect Eleanor to—'

'Are we going to fight over her?' Alanna asked, her calm voice hardly masking her anger.

'I hope not. Because she's the one that will

suffer most. But you have to remember, I love her as much as I'm sure you will learn to do and—'

His mobile phone rang. His mobile—that meant it would be important. Only a few people had this number. This was the worst possible time—but he had to reply.

'Dr Cavendish?' He recognised the voice at once. Mike Thornton, who ran a large agricultural supplies business. He was also the leader and organiser of the local mountain rescue team. And this was business, otherwise Mike would have called him Finn.

'What's the problem, Mike?'

'Are you available now? We've got what might be a bad one. Though it won't take too much time.'

Finn thought quickly. He had an arrangement with the cottage hospital and the practice that, if he was needed for a rescue, then he would be released from whatever duties he had—if it was at all possible. And now he was technically not at work at all. But could he leave Alanna here on her own? Mike was usually right so this shouldn't take too much time. There'd be enough time to do the rescue and then get back in time to pick up Eleanor. 'What's the problem?' he asked.

'Couple of walkers on Baleda Fell. They seem to be quite expert, both know what they are doing. But the woman slipped on a rocky bit and rolled quite a way. She's got bruises and is bleeding from a not too bad head wound. But she's hurt her back and has lost the feeling in one leg.'

Finn winced. It could be nothing. But there might also be a broken spine. And if she was moved badly, there might be irreversible paralysis.

Mike must have guessed his thoughts. 'Her boyfriend is clued up. He knows not to move her and I know exactly where they are. I said we'll be there as soon as possible. Just half a dozen of us and the Bell stretcher. Ideally I'd like you to supervise lifting her onto the stretcher.'

'Good idea.' The Bell stretcher was taken out on every rescue mission. It was lightweight but tremendously strong. Patients could be strapped to it so there was no danger of movement and carried over the roughest of terrain. 'Count me in. Come and pick me up,' Finn said. 'How many rescuers have you got so far?'

'With you, five. I'm ringing around and—'

'I'm at home, so pick me up here. And I've got a sixth member here.'

There was surprise in Mike's voice. 'Who's that?'

'You don't know her. But she's a mountaineer and a trained A and E nurse.'

'Be round at yours in ten minutes.' Mike rang off.

Finn looked at Alanna, who had been quite unashamedly listening to the conversation. 'There's a mountain rescue,' he said. 'I've just volunteered you.'

She looked at him blank-faced, saying nothing.

'I'm thinking as a doctor,' he said. 'I think it might be a good idea if right now you had some hard physical exercise. You've just been through a shattering experience and later on you're going to go through another when you hold her for the first time. A hard time on the mountain will settle you a little. But it's your choice.'

He saw that she was thinking, considering. 'You're making decisions for me,' she said. 'That's not the best of ideas so don't get into the habit. But perhaps it would be good for me to go. I've got walking kit in my rucksack—shall I change now?'

'Good idea. I'll do the same.' Then, daring, he said, 'But you look well in the nurse's uniform.'

'I like wearing it,' she said.

For a moment in the bathroom she had wondered just why she was doing this. Of course, it was the thing that she did, this was similar to rescues she had been on a dozen times in the past four years. But she had just heard… as she thought of it her head started to reel with the possibilities, the thought of what emotions were to come. And then she'd decided he was right. She needed physical exercise.

She had liked wearing the nurse's uniform, it had been a while since she had worn one. She felt it gave her a status, made her feel professional. Of course, over the past few years she had occasionally been given a uniform. But mostly she had worn what had been suitable for the temperature and the terrain.

She went back to the bathroom to change, to put on sturdy walking gear, her boots. When she came out he was dressed similarly. He was carrying a heavy rucksack, she knew it would hold a medical kit. So far today she had seen him in what seemed to be typical country doctor's clothes—half formal, half comfortable. There was a light jacket, checked shirt, a pleasant enough tie. But now he was different. Changing clothes had changed his character.

Seeing him dressed like this made her feel…well, odd. They had walked together a lot when they'd been young. His appearance brought back memories that she was not sure that she wanted right now. She saw him looking at her, saw the flash of recognition, of memory in his eyes too. Perhaps also there was a look of regret.

She had wrapped a clean bandana round her neck—a black and white checked one. He said, 'You always used to wear something like that. I used to tell you that you wanted to be a cowboy.'

She grinned. 'I did want to be a cowboy. And for a while, in Argentina, I was one. A cowgirl nurse.'

'What a mixture.'

From outside there came the sound of a horn. They walked out, there was a long-wheelbase Land Rover—she recognised it as the kind adapted for this kind of work. She climbed in and the vehicle was moving before Finn had shut the door. There were quick introductions to the four men there, she took to them at once. She recognised the type. She had been among them for most of her life.

Finn chatted casually, jokingly to the four as they drove out into the country. She was rather surprised. This was a man who was at home in the community. Who knew everyone, was interested in everyone. Who was interested in their lives, not just their injuries. She thought how different he had been from when he was an aspiring A and E registrar, hoping to make consultant in the quickest time ever.

She glanced out of the window—it was country she knew. She was surprised how much it affected her. Why, there was a peak where she and Finn had… Then it came back to her with a jerk. What she had just been told. She had a daughter!

She couldn't help it. Just once, she sobbed.

Finn looked at her assessingly. 'Are you OK? Mike's driving not too bumpy for you?'

'I've been in Land Rovers before,' she said. 'And over rougher ground than this.'

She had been in tight situations before as well. But never one as tough as the one she was to face later that afternoon.

Baleda Fell was about five miles away. Mike obviously knew the ground well. They turned off the narrow road onto a rough track and then parked at the foot of a steep rise. The five men were well practiced and were out of the vehicle at once, grabbing their equipment stashed in the back. And then they were climbing a steep narrow path, moving fast but not hurrying.

'You all right with this pace?' Mike asked after a quarter of an hour.

'If I get tired, you can leave me behind.' At times, a touch of sarcasm was a good thing.

'I doubt that'll be necessary.'

After a while they left the path and zig-zagged

up a steep fell. They came to a small rockface, scrambled up it. The man ahead of her turned and offered her a hand.

She just looked at him, then scampered up the rock past him. He grinned sheepishly.

Eventually they came to the couple who had asked for help. The man was kneeling, white-faced, by the supine body of the girl. 'Thank God you've come,' he gasped. 'It might be nothing but I just don't know.' The detached part of Alanna's mind had to approve what he had done. He had immobilised the girl, kept her warm and waited. Waiting was often the hardest part.

Mike said, 'Well, we're here now so you can stop worrying. I'm Mike Thornton, head of this mountain rescue team. And you are?'

'I'm Peter Brown, this is Mary Dancer. She's my... fiancée. We've just got engaged. This holiday was meant to be a celebration. Great way to celebrate.'

'We can sort things out, Peter,' Mike said. 'Don't worry. This kind of thing can happen all the time. Now, come over here and sit down. Have a hot drink.'

Alanna nodded to herself. Good rescue technique. Reassure people, make them feel they're among friends. Shock could hit people even on the warmest day. This would help Peter.

Meanwhile Finn had knelt next to the recumbent girl and motioned Alanna to kneel opposite him. Peter had done everything properly—there was a space blanket wrapped tightly round the girl, an extra anorak covering her. On her head was a blood-stained balaclava. Apparently a rough dressing was underneath.

Finn took the girl's hand. 'Hi Mary,' he said. 'I'm Dr Cavendish and these men are going to carry you down off the hillside. Then we're going to the hospital where I'll examine you properly. But first let's put this on.' He had already taken a hard collar from the pack. Alanna lifted the head gently while he slipped it on and fastened it.

A quick medical check followed. Mary was breathing well, her circulation seemed fine. Finn checked the rest of her body for hidden injuries. Then, gently, he slipped a hand underneath her, felt the spine for tenderness, deformity, a 'step' in the spinal column. He was reasonably hopeful as he could find obvious injury.

When he had finished he asked Alanna to look at the head wound, put a temporary dressing on it. Then he rose to talk quietly to Peter. Alanna knew what he was doing—trying to find out exactly how Mary had fallen, what had happened.

The medical kit was open. Alanna pulled on a pair of rubber gloves and then gently eased the balaclava back. She had seen Finn check Mary's eyes for uneven dilation of the pupils but there was none. She winced as she saw the gash—some of Mary's hair would have to come off to suture it. But for the moment it was a matter of stabilizing things. Alanna took a compression pad from the kit, fixed it tightly on top of the still bleeding cut then replaced the balaclava. It would hold until they got to the hospital. She looked up at Finn and nodded. 'I've finished here,' she said.

The stretcher had already been assembled and laid by Mary's side. Finn took her head, the four men knelt by her, lifted her according to Finn's instructions and placed her gently on the stretcher. Then they left Finn to strap her in. Time to get back to the Land Rover.

It was different going down. There were four men handling the stretcher. To begin with she and Finn were left out, which was good as it would give Finn time to assess Peter, make sure that he wasn't in shock.

But she said to Mike, 'We rotate, OK? I do my share of carrying the stretcher.'

'Have you carried a stretcher over rough ground before?'

'More than anyone here, I suspect.'

Mike looked at her for a moment and then said, 'OK, we rotate.'

And they did rotate. She let the four men slide the stretcher down the rocky stretch, using the ropes provided. This was something they had practised as a team. But on the flatter ground she took her turn.

The stretcher was slotted carefully into the Land Rover, Finn made another swift check on their patient and then they were heading for the hospital. Alanna noticed that Mike was driving carefully so Mary's neck wasn't jolted too much.

Finn used his mobile to call Rosewood, and talked to Stella, the matron. Together they decided that Mary should be taken to the cottage hospital. At present there was no need to send for an ambulance to take her to Carlisle. 'Get us a bed ready,' Finn said, 'and turn out the radiographer. We'll want pictures of her spine. I'll need her in Theatre to suture her scalp but I don't think there'll be any need for an anaesthetist.'

This was the old Finn—clear, purposeful, concentrating solely on the matter in hand. Alanna realised that she had done what he had—lost herself in the search and rescue. Unbelievably, she had forgotten—or pushed to the back of her mind—the news she had been given, but now it came rushing back.

She was going to the cottage hospital where her daughter was in the crèche.

'Are we going straight to Rosewood?' she asked Finn.

He looked at her face, guessed what she was feeling. 'You'll be OK,' he said. 'You're tough.'

Did she want to be tough?

* * *

The vehicle rolled onto the forecourt of Rosewood and she felt—How did she feel? There was a turmoil of emotions—she was happy, shocked, apprehensive, bewildered. What would happen next? Then she decided. Finn was right, she was tough. Or at least she'd act as if she was tough. She had so much to fight for. Fight for? Was she going to have to fight for her daughter? Well, yes, if it was necessary.

Then she thought of Finn. No, it was too much, she couldn't cope with thinking about Eleanor and of Finn. She allowed herself just one fleeting idea. She had enjoyed being with him.

She was not yet an official nurse, she had no position at the hospital. She had to stand by and watch as the injured girl was carefully lifted out of the Land Rover and carried inside. She watched Peter filling in forms for the booking-in nurse, saw that Mary had to sign a consent form.

Finn went to shower and change into something more suitable for a hospital doctor. But first he came over to her. 'With any luck this should only take an hour, an hour and a half,' he said. 'You go upstairs. There's a nurses'-doctors' room there, you can read magazines, have a coffee, take things easy. I'll be with you as soon as I can. The nurse here will take you.'

The transformation had taken place. The rural, easygoing doctor had disappeared, once more he was the focussed A and E man, thinking solely of his patient. 'I'll wait for you there,' she said.

She wondered if he'd believe her. But there was only a curt nod and he disappeared.

A friendly nurse took her upstairs, made sure she was comfortable and had enough magazines to keep her occupied for a week and showed her how to work the coffee-machine. Then she, too, disappeared.

Alanna drank the coffee she had made herself. Then she went next door to where the nurse had told her was the ladies' cloakroom. She washed her face, dragged a comb through her hair. She looked at herself in the mirror, decided that she didn't look too bad. Then she realised what she was doing. She was afraid. She was about to take a step that would alter her life.

She went downstairs, turned left down a corridor. Well, if challenged, she could say that she was looking for the ladies. She knew there'd be one on every floor. This was an old house, but since she had last visited it there had been another wing built on. She didn't know where anything was. There were various signs pointing to different departments, but no sign showing the way to the crèche. What if she just couldn't find it?

She stood still, listened. There was the mumble of voices, the slap of feet on hard wooden floors. Then she heard it. Childish voices singing. She turned down a side corridor, following the sound, and came to a door. She opened it a crack.

There were a dozen or so children sitting on the floor, gazing up at a young woman who was reading to them. The children were singing or cheering or shouting when certain words came up. They seemed to be enjoying it.

She looked from child to child, opened the door a crack more. There, on the right of the teacher, was…her daughter.

She was wearing a little blue dress, she had dark hair, she was smiling. Alanna felt her heart beat as it had never beaten before. Her daughter. So beautiful.

She couldn't help it, she pushed the door open a bit more. The woman reading saw the movement, closed her book and came over, smiling. 'You must be lost,' she said. 'May I help?'

Then her smiled faded and she frowned as Alanna stood there, completely unable to speak.

But then she gained control of herself. She remembered her cover story. 'Sorry,' she gabbled, 'I got lost, I've been looking for the ladies. I'm waiting for Dr Cavendish—we've just been on a rescue together.'

'Oh, right. I heard the team was bringing someone in. Everyone safe, then?'

'We hope so. There's a girl being treated right now.' Alanna licked her dry lips. She mumbled, 'Everyone seems to be enjoying themselves in here.'

'This is the best job in the hospital,' the young woman said, 'I'd better get back to it. By the way, the ladies is down that corridor and on the left.'

For a moment Alanna thought of asking if she could stay and watch, but then thought better of it. There would be questions. So she thanked the woman and walked down the corridor towards the cloakroom. She was aware that she was being watched so she turned into the cloakroom. Best not to arouse suspicions.

She'd washed her face not ten minutes ago. No point in doing it again, so she contented herself with gazing into the mirror. Her face looked like a stranger's. No longer was it the old, confident, perhaps remote face of a woman who was in charge of herself and her destiny. Now she looked unsure, vulnerable.

Rubbish! She could cope. She had to. She went back upstairs, threw away the half-cup of coffee she had left and made herself another.

Finn came into the room an hour or so later. He was still in scrubs and looked a little tired. She poured him a coffee and then asked, 'How is the patient?'

He sipped his coffee and smiled. 'She's good. Her back seems OK according to the X-ray. I suspect the muscles just went into spasm. She's recovering feeling in her leg. There's a consultant coming down tomorrow for a clinic, he'll have a look at it. Her head was a bit of a mess but I've sutured the cut and her hair will grow back. In all, she's a lucky girl.'

He swirled his coffee around in his cup, looked at her a moment. Then he said, 'I gather you've been for a bit of a wander around. Lucy from the crèche phoned up about you. She's cautious about strange people who look in who have no apparent business there.'

'I'm impressed, I think that's a good thing,' said Alanna, and meant it. He was still looking at her in a mildly accusing way but he said nothing. So she added, 'All right, I went to see my daughter! I just couldn't resist, with her being in the same building.'

'And…?'

'Finn, she's lovely!'

He nodded. 'She is. I can see you in her face— you have the same cheekbones, the same wonderful eyes. But now you've seen her, and feel satisfied she's your daughter, how do you feel?'

She had to confess. 'Still lost. But determined.'

'That's understandable.' He looked at his

watch. 'It's an hour before I usually pick her up, but there's no point in going home and then coming back for her. So we'll take her now. I haven't got a car here, but Stella Martin has offered to run us home.'

'Us?'

'You, me and Eleanor. Alanna, I've been thinking about this. How would it be if we tell Eleanor that you're an old friend of mine and that you'll be staying with us for a while? She can call you Auntie Alanna.'

'But I'm her mother!'

'That will have to come in time,' he said gently. 'And it will. But for now, are you happy with the arrangement?'

Alanna gasped. She hadn't had much time to think about the practicalities. This seemed a good start. 'I'm to stay with you?' she asked.

'For the moment, yes. The three of us are going to have to do some serious thinking.'

'The three of us,' she repeated. 'Yes, we will.'

CHAPTER FIVE

ALANNA felt a sense of unreality. Finn went to change and then she was taken back down to the crèche and formally introduced to Lucy there. 'This is Alanna, a very old friend of mine. In fact, we grew up together here. She'll be staying with me for a while, so if she ever comes to pick Eleanor up that'll be fine.'

Lucy looked at her with obvious curiosity but said nothing. She went to fetch Eleanor's coat and lunchbox. Alanna realised that as an explanation what Finn had said left a lot to be desired. Much more would have to be said in time. But what?

Then she looked across the room. A little face peered from behind a box of toys, and then a blue-clad figure hurtling across the room. 'Daddy, Daddy, Daddy!'

Finn picked up their child, whirled her

around. Then he said, 'This is Auntie Alanna Eleanor. She's going to stay with us for a while. Give her a kiss.'

He held the child out to Alanna who took her into her arms and stared speechlessly at her daughter. She felt warm skin, the tickle of hair on her cheek. She tried to look at Eleanor's face but tears blurred her eyes. Then she felt arms around her neck, felt the tiniest of kisses on her cheek. ''Lo, Auntie Alanna,' a little voice said.

Alanna wanted to hug her, hug her hard. But this was a little girl in her arms so she contented herself with just a little squeeze. Finn must have realised what was happening, how she was feeling, so he took her by the arm and guided her down the corridor. They went to where a car was waiting, its engine running. Finn performed a quick introduction and then said, 'Give Eleanor to me. Stella has a child of her own so there's a child seat in the back.'

He took Eleanor and started to fasten her in. Alanna saw Stella looking at her, knew that her tears were showing. So she said, 'I think I must have got something in my eye.' Well, it was some sort of an explanation, if not a good one.

Finn showed her into the back seat next to Eleanor. He sat in the front. And as the car pulled away Alanna stared at the little girl who was her daughter.

Eleanor stared back at her thoughtfully then apparently decided that Alanna was all right. She undid the lunchbox on her lap and took out a piece of paper. 'We did finger painting today,' she said. 'I did this one. It's birds in the sky.'

Alanna looked at the piece of paper. 'It's very good,' she said. 'Are you going to ask your… daddy if you can put it on the wall?'

'On the fridge,' Eleanor confided. 'We've got magnets that stick things onto the fridge.'

Alanna couldn't help stroking the bare arms, feeling the warmth. She had missed all this for four years, it just wasn't fair. But the future was…the future was going to be good.

When they arrived at Finn's house. Alanna stood to one side as Finn unbuckled Eleanor—though she would have liked to have done it herself. They waved goodbye to Stella and went into the house.

'I'm going in my Wendy house,' said Eleanor, and bolted across the room.

'Well, was that hard?' a gentle voice by her side asked. And now she knew she could let the tears flow.

'Hard? Hard? Finn, all those wasted years. When I held her I wanted to… Come here, I need…' She rushed to him, wrapped her arms so hard around him that she knew he would feel the discomfort. 'This hug isn't for you,' she wept, 'this is for me and what I feel for that little girl and for all the emotions I'm feeling that I just can't get my head around and I need to hold somebody.'

There was one arm around her waist, another stroked the back of her neck. 'All will be well,' he said. 'All will be well.' He kissed her on the cheek, a kiss of comfort. 'You must give it time.'

They stood together for quite some time. And then she felt her racing heart slowing and she slowly came to her senses. A new small thought intruded, a new feeling. All her thoughts so far had been for herself and for Eleanor. But now she realised she was hugging—and being hugged by—the man she had come there to divorce. Her nearly ex-husband, the man with whom she'd had those rows, the man she had vowed to cast out of her life. And she was rather enjoying the hugging. And the being hugged.

Unexpected memories drifted back, of when they had been happy together. They had laughed together, joked together, felt they could read each other's minds. They had been the most passionate of lovers. But those times were gone!

She released him, stepped back. 'Sorry,' she said. 'I'm not usually a hysterical woman.'

'You're not hysterical at all,' he said. 'One thing I have learned is that it's good to let your emotions show.'

She didn't want to think about that. 'I want to go and play with Eleanor,' she said. 'Just want to be with her and watch her. I know that there's a lot of talking to be done, a lot of decisions to be made.'

She took a breath, forced herself to talk calmly. 'You've been so good to me today Finn, but let's face it, we parted swearing that if we never met again, it would be too soon.'

His face hardened. 'I remember,' he said. 'And we both meant it. But for now, for this evening, let's declare a truce. At the weekend we'll have to talk, talk hard. But I know what you're feeling now and I wouldn't deny my worst enemy the pleasure you're going to have. Go and play with her. Tell her that as a special treat the two of you can have tea together in the Wendy house. And, Alanna, remember she's only four and—'

'I know what you're going to say. Keep my own feelings back. I'm not to ask her to call me Mummy, not hold her too much. Treat her like any other friend's little girl, don't upset her with too much emotion. I can do all that. But, Finn, I've got so much time to make up!'

'I know. Well. I'll bring you both tea in half an hour and…' Then he grinned and said, 'But do you want to shower again and change first? The rescue was quite a sweaty one.'

'A polite way of suggesting that I smell?' she asked and looked down at her creased clothing. 'Yes, I guess I would like to change.'

He thought for a moment. 'Top of the stairs, first on the left. There's a guest bedroom and it has its own bathroom. Take your rucksack up there, it can be your room.'

She nodded. 'OK. Incidentally, where does Eleanor sleep?'

'My bedroom had a dressing room leading off it. I converted it into a tiny nursery. I like her to be near me. But in a year or two she'll move into her own bedroom. She's growing up.'

'Growing up,' said Alanna.

She took her bag upstairs, found the guest bedroom. She liked it. When they had lived together in a flat in Leeds it had been—not spartan but very impersonal. Both of them had been working so hard that there had been little time to furnish, to decorate, to work out the best way of running the place. And over her last four years of wandering, she had usually been glad just to have a bed, an insect-free room and running water.

This room was welcoming. It still had a masculine touch. The walls may have been painted a pastel rose shade, but the bedspread and upholstery were both a rich burgundy. There was no excessive ornamentation, the pictures were of mountain scenes. Yes, she liked the room. Though if it was hers, she'd alter it a bit. She'd have… What was she thinking of?

She decided to take his advice, have another shower. She'd enjoyed the rescue, but it had been warm.

The bathroom was comfortable, too. Towels were ready on a shelf, together with an expensive soap. She had a long luxurious shower and then looked—no shampoo. No matter, she had a bottle of her own particular favourite in her rucksack, she'd just run and get it. She opened the bathroom door, decided there was no need of a protective towel for the two paces to reach the rucksack she had left open on the bed.

Wrong decision. Wet through and stark naked, she stepped into the bedroom. And there was Finn, dropping sheets onto the bed.

Her first reaction was every woman's. To cross her hands protectively over her breasts. Her arms did move but then she forced them to stay by her sides.

'Oh, sorry. I did knock but you were in the shower and you can't have heard,' he said, em-

barrassed. 'I was just dropping these off and…
I'll go now.'

'Nothing you haven't seen before,' she said.

He didn't reply, merely left the room.

She found her shampoo, went back into the
bathroom. There she looked at herself in the
full-length mirror. All right, she was being
immodest. But she didn't look at all bad.

She had noticed that Finn hadn't stared at her,
but neither had he looked away. She wondered
what his reaction to her body had been. She
wondered at her own reaction. She'd been quite
pleased that he had seen her.

In various nursing jobs throughout the world
she had sometimes had to entertain children,
play with them. Often it had been hard because
they'd spoken a different language to her.

It hadn't been the part of the job that she had
enjoyed most. It brought back memories, possibilities. But she was a professional, so she had
done it as best she could.

She had never envisaged playing with her own
daughter. There was a plastic red and yellow

Wendy house. Lined up against the back wall was a set of dolls. There was just enough room inside for her and Eleanor to sit cross-legged, facing each other. The dolls were having their tea. They had their own set of plastic cutlery and crockery, and they all had names.

After half an hour there was a knock on the outside door. 'Is anybody at home in Eleanor's house?'

When invited to enter, Finn pushed two trays into the little room. On one was a plate of cut-up salmon and salad, a fruit salad and a glass of milk. On the other was a sandwich and a mug of tea.

'Having tea together in here is very nice, isn't it?' asked Eleanor as she started on her salad. 'Sometimes I have it in here with Daddy, except that he has to sit outside 'cos there's not enough room.'

'He's a big daddy,' Alanna agreed.

Afterwards she and Finn bathed Eleanor and then Finn asked if Alanna could read a story instead of him. Eleanor agreed. But it had to be Daddy who sat with her until she was fully asleep.

He had refused Alana's offer of help in the

kitchen. He told her that the meal was already prepared, it would only take ten minutes to serve it. So she sat in his living room, jumping from channel to channel on the television, finding nothing she wanted to watch. There was a bookshelf in the corner, she wandered over to it—and there on the top were a couple of photograph albums.

She flicked through the first. Pictures of Eleanor, aged two onwards. Tears welled again as she saw what she had been missing. She seemed to have wept more today than in the past five years.

Then there was the second album. She recognised it, it was of their marriage. It was a moment before she took it up and opened it. Was there much point? Still—she was curious. There weren't many pictures. It had been a casual, spur-of-the-moment thing. She looked at herself, laughing at Finn. Kissing him in the middle of a Leeds street, wearing jeans and a bride's veil. It had only been five, six years ago. What had happened to that careless, happy girl?

She put the album on the couch, went over to

a mirror on the wall and looked at herself. Her face was still the same—a little thinner perhaps, but obviously recognisable. The features hadn't changed. What might have changed was what was written on the face. Now she looked more… Cautious? Wary?

She looked at Finn's pictures. He had changed, too, but not in the same way. He used to look intense, determined. Now his face was easier, more relaxed.

She heard him enter the room behind her. She turned and asked rather bitterly, 'Do you often look at pictures of our happy married life?'

He didn't rise to her bitterness. 'Sometimes,' he said. He took the album from her, open at a page showing the two of them, arms around each other's waists, laughing at the camera. 'Look at us,' he said. 'Apparently grown-up but we were children. What harm we did to each other.'

'Right. But that's in the past now.'

Together they looked at the picture in silence. Then he snapped the album shut and said, 'Dinner's ready. You must be starving.'

They ate in the kitchen. They started with salad

and shrimps in a marie-rose sauce, the shrimps from the Morecambe Bay estuary some twenty miles away. Then a wonderful shepherd's pie with fresh turnips and carrots. He poured her a glass of red wine. After a second helping of the shepherd's pie and a second glass of red wine she told him that no way could she eat any cheese or fruit, no matter how good it looked.

'Then let's go into the living room and I'll fetch us coffee in a moment.'

'That'll be nice. Then we can…' She couldn't help it. As they walked through to the living room she yawned, a great, body-stretching yawn. But it wasn't that late!

Finn smiled as they sat side by side on his couch. 'Tired?' he asked. 'This has been a long day for you.'

'Emotion is more tiring than exercise,' she told him, 'and I've had both. Finn, this has been the most…most shattering day of my life. My world has been turned upside down. What I knew this morning isn't true any more. All my priorities have changed.' She thought for a moment. 'In fact, I didn't have any priorities, I was a free agent. Finn, I don't know where to start. There are decisions to be made, and I'm lost.'

'I don't want to talk yet either,' he said. 'I know the bigger shock has been yours—but you just dropping into my life again, it's shocked me, too. I suspect you're going to change things. Now, I'll fetch the coffee-pot.'

There was silence while he fetched the coffee, poured them both some. The she felt she had to speak. 'There's just one thing I have to say. Now I know I've got a daughter I'm going to be a proper mother. My daughter is going to be the centre of my life from now on.'

'She already is the centre of my life,' he told her quietly.

'Well, that's fine but—'

He held up his hand. 'I have a suggestion. Today is Wednesday. This weekend I have free. You stay here with Eleanor and me, try to get to know her better. Wait until your emotions settle a bit—though I can tell you, it'll take quite a time. Saturday night we'll have a talk, quietly and calmly, and try to decide about the future. See what we can sort out.'

'Fine. Just so long as you understand that—'

'Alanna!' His voice was sharp. 'Remember where talking like that got us last time. Only this time something more precious is at stake.'

'True,' she muttered after a pause. 'For the moment I think I'd better just keep quiet.'

They sat together in more or less amicable silence for a while and then she said, 'It's been a…hard day. I think I need to go to bed early.'

'Me, too.'

She looked at him. He did look tired. So she said, 'I've been thinking only of myself, haven't I? Well, myself and Eleanor, that is. But I suppose this must have been very hard for you, too.'

'You could say that. I did try very hard to find you after I first heard about Eleanor. But there was no response and so I guess I more or less gave up on you. I was content in my life so why should I worry? Now, shall we both go to bed?'

They made a few general arrangements about the next day and then he smiled and said, 'I know what you want now. You want to go and look at Eleanor asleep.'

She nodded. 'Of course I do.'

So they went through his bedroom and looked at the sleeping child. Finn straightened the sheet on her, then stooped to kiss her forehead. Alanna kissed her, too. The little form wriggled, there was a half-heard gasp. Time to leave.

As they tiptoed out of the bedroom Alanna wiped yet more tears from her eyes and said, 'You know I don't cry. Well, today I have.' She thought a moment and went on, 'And in a shocking way, perhaps I've been happier than at any time in my life before. Well, not happy, but…' Words failed her.

It didn't matter. 'I know exactly what you mean. The shock's too much. And it'll last for quite a few days. But then you'll know how your life is different.'

She went to her bedroom, undressed and knew that her exhausted body would soon be asleep. There was one last thought, and it was of Finn, not Eleanor. He had changed. No, he hadn't. He was still the same—but he had changed as well. She felt the tiniest upsurge of the feelings she'd once had for him. Then she slept.

* * *

It was sunny again the next day and she wandered around Benthwaite. It hadn't changed too much, though she had. This had been her home, she had loved it. She had climbed— usually with Finn—every hill within sight. But at the same time she'd had the urge to wander. To see what was beyond the next hill. And the hill after that and the sea after that. She had set off when she was eighteen. It had been hard to say goodbye to the place and also to Finn, her childhood sweetheart. Still, both of them had agreed in one of their more sober moments that parting for a while might be the right thing to do. She sat on a bench, gazed at the distant peaks and thought of what had happened afterwards.

Finn had gone to medical school—what he had always wanted to do. She had gone abroad to do charity work on Africa. After the year in Africa she had wandered further. For a while they had written to each other—and then the letters had petered out.

She had been away for three years. But then she'd come back to Leeds, looked up Finn and it had been as if she had never been away. For another three years she'd trained to be a nurse. Then she'd qualified, and they'd got married. In a hurry. In those days they'd done everything in a hurry.

He had been the ambitious young doctor who'd wanted to specialise in A and E in a big city hospital. She had been the nurse working with him. They had been happy, the world there to be enjoyed, nothing could go wrong. And they'd decided to have a baby.

Alanna flinched. That was when their charmed life had started to go wrong. She didn't want to think about it any more.

Things were so different now. In one pocket she felt the weight of a mobile phone. She had bought it a fortnight ago when she had first come back to England. They were so useful. She wished she'd had one in many of the places she had been abroad. They would have been really useful there. But that had been then. She had given Finn her number in case there were any changes in their plans.

Yes, Benthwaite hadn't changed much. There were some new houses, a couple of shops had changed, the car park had been extended. She saw a few faces that she recognised, but for the most part tried to avoid looking at people. Meeting them would have to come in time and it would cause a few problems. But she was happy there.

She'd had fun having breakfast with Eleanor. Boiled egg with soldiers. Finn had drawn a face on Eleanor's egg, and she had insisted that Alanna and Finn had faces, too.

They'd agreed—reluctantly on Alana's part— not to disturb Eleanor's normal routine. She had gone to the crèche as usual. Alanna had wanted to keep her at home for the day, said she would walk round the town with her daughter. But Finn had been against it. Best not to alter the routine too much. Alanna had felt he was wrong but for once managed to keep her feelings to herself. Finn had gone into work. 'I've got hospital rounds this morning, in the surgery this afternoon. What do you intend to do?'

'I'll wander around town. Perhaps see if people here remember me.'

'What are you going to say if you meet an old friend?'

'Dunno. I'm confused.' Perhaps it was as well that she didn't have Eleanor with her.

They had agreed to meet at the hospital at five, then she could drive home with Finn and Eleanor. In the meantime, Finn had given her a key to his house, which she thought was good of him. It was an unexpected gesture, it seemed trusting and hospitable. If she wished, she could go back there and rest.

But for the moment she was happy just to wander around Benthwaite. Yesterday had been so emotionally fraught. It was good to have nothing to worry about, no new problems to consider.

She had a daughter! When she thought that, the very idea filled her with a joy beyond imagining. But was it a problem? Well, yes, in some ways it was.

She walked around for three or four hours. Then she phoned Finn's surgery and asked if it would be possible to see Dr Matthews at some time—no, not a medical consultation, a personal matter. She was invited to call at lunchtime.

As she replaced the receiver Alanna felt a mixture of trepidation and satisfaction. Yesterday had been wonderful—but it had largely consisted of things being revealed to her, done to and for her. Now she was trying to make decisions of her own.

She sat in the same little room that she had been in yesterday. The same receptionist brought in a tray of coffee. But how her life had altered since then!

Sitting opposite her was Dr Harry Matthews. A big man, over six feet three and heavy-shouldered. His hair was now entirely white, but was as thick as ever. He must be in his late fifties by now, she thought. He smiled at her imperturbably. At first he looked to be a simple country doctor. But she knew that the amiable exterior hid a complex mind.

'I called on you yesterday to try to find out where Finn might be,' she told him. 'I thought that meeting him would be something simple, a bit of business that could be over in an hour. An episode in my life that needed closure. You're an old friend, you helped both Finn and me when we were younger. You said you'd arrange a meeting and you also offered me a job—which I thought was a laugh. By the way, is the job offer still open?'

'It is. If my partners agree to it.'

'Why did you offer me a job?'

As calmly as ever he said, 'Because we need someone urgently and you're ideally qualified.'

'Harry! You know very well that there are…reasons why it's going to be awkward. You knew about Eleanor being my daughter. Why didn't you tell me?'

'Because that was something that you and Finn had to sort out yourselves. I didn't tell you about Eleanor and I didn't tell him that you were the one who might take on the job. You needed to get together without any preconceptions.'

'Preconceptions! Harry, I got the biggest shock of my life. I'm still shaking with it, still trying to grasp the consequences. To make sense of things. I'm wildly happy. But I'm also scared.'

'A very understandable reaction,' Harry said. 'Alanna, there's no need to hurry to make any decisions. I offered you the job because I thought it might give you a breathing space. Time to sort things out between you and Finn.'

'We parted four years ago, Harry! Living together had become such hell that we were both glad to get away. There's nothing to sort out between Finn and me. It's already been done.'

'So I understand,' Harry said placidly. 'But now things are different. You have a daughter and you have to share her.'

'I think Finn and I have gone beyond the sharing stage. But one thing is certain. Now I've found her I'm never going to be parted from Eleanor again.'

'That's reasonable. The trouble is, I'm sure Finn would say exactly the same thing.' He paused and then said, 'Of course, I see a lot of fathers in my job. Some are bad, some are good, some just do as well as they can. But I can honestly say that Finn is one of the most devoted fathers I've ever come across. He might think he's a lucky man, having Eleanor. In time Eleanor will come to find that she's a lucky girl, having Finn.'

'Are you trying to warn me off, Harry?'

He looked shocked. 'Not at all. I'm just offering facts—opinions perhaps—for you to take into consideration. Finn has changed, Alanna. Have you changed?'

She thought about that. 'To be honest, I haven't changed enough, I suppose. I'm still as single-minded as ever. And I've never stuck to one job for long.'

'That's not good enough for a mother. Children need continuity.'

'Then I'll change,' she told him. 'Being a mother is a job that I can stick to.'

The rest of the day passed like a dream. Alanna found that she didn't need to see Eleanor all the time—the very fact that she had a daughter was good enough for her. She had to get used to the idea. Harry had said she would have to change. Well, she could do it.

She found herself passing a shop that sold children's clothes and glanced casually in the window. Ordinarily—to be exact, until yesterday—it would have held no interest for her. But now she stopped and stared, entranced. She saw a little set of overalls in a shade of blue that would go well with Eleanor's hair and skin. There was a penguin embroidered on the front. Perhaps she could suggest to Finn that… Why should she suggest to Finn?

She was about to enter the shop when something stopped her. A memory of the last time she had shopped for children's clothes. She had bought a layette for their unborn baby. And when she had discovered that there was no baby she had given it, untouched, to a charity shop.

She stepped away from the shop, feeling anger grow inside her. It wasn't fair! She had suffered so much and… But now things were different. She must look to the future.

She turned again, went into the shop and came out with a small pink wrapped parcel.

CHAPTER SIX

THURSDAY evening passed much as Wednesday evening had. She met Finn at Rosewood at five then she and Finn went down to the crèche to pick up Eleanor and received more curious looks from Lucy. Then she played with Eleanor in the Wendy house again, had tea with her, then later on the bath and bedtime story. It was hard not to reach for her daughter all the time, to hug her as if she would never let her go. But Alanna managed. And she knew that every minute she was falling more and more in love with the little girl.

She had decided to be cautious with Finn. After they had had tea together she told him, 'I hope you don't mind but I've bought something for Eleanor. I was passing a shop and I just couldn't resist.' She unwrapped the parcel held up the overalls for him to see. 'Aren't these just gorgeous?'

'Gorgeous,' he agreed. 'She'll look lovely in them.' But there was a lack of enthusiasm in his voice.

She looked at him reproachfully. 'Finn, all mothers love dressing their children. Especially little girls. I haven't been able to do it before, you wouldn't begrudge me that pleasure?'

He laughed. 'You're right, of course. It's just that…I've always bought her clothes so far. And I've enjoyed it, Someone else doing what I think is my job—well, it takes a bit of getting used to.'

'You'll get used to me quite quickly,' she said.

He looked at her, his eyes serious. 'Will I? I think you'll be a good mother to Eleanor. But she has a father, too. How are you going to deal with him?'

For a moment the question hovered between them. It was like a precipice—neither wanted to walk near the edge but both of them knew that in time it would be necessary.

She decided that she had to say something. 'I came here just to see you,' she said. 'My idea was to get things sorted out, if you hadn't already divorced me, then to offer you the chance to do so. But then we met, and after that initial shock and distrust I saw bits of you that I had half forgotten. I remembered why we had been so attracted to each other. I felt easier with you. When we went on your rounds, when we went on that rescue. I felt that I was living in the past, and the past was good. But now there's Eleanor. And I'm wondering how she will… well, will she bring us closer together or drive us further apart?' She paused, her face troubled. 'What do you think?'

He frowned, shook his head as if trying to clear it. 'We can't just forget Eleanor exists. But when we first met—like you, after the initial shock, I remembered why I'd first fallen in love with you.'

Things were moving too quickly for Alanna. 'Just a first impression,' she said, 'on both our parts.'

He retreated equally quickly. 'Just a first impression,' he agreed. 'But, Alanna, even when we parted…it might have been the only thing for you to do but I loved you still, even if I couldn't make you see it. When you'd gone, when I finally realised that you weren't coming back, I tried to put you out of my mind. But I never quite managed it.'

'Me neither, I suppose,' she mumbled after a while. 'And now I'm just…confused.'

They looked at each other and somehow both decided that now wasn't the time. There was an unspoken agreement, for the moment they would wait and see. 'Things will work out,' she said. 'We'll come to some kind of arrangement.'

'I'm sure we will.' And that was that. For the moment.

Next day was Friday. Another enjoyable breakfast, then Finn went to work and Alanna was left on her own again for the day. But this time she didn't wander casually around the little town. Instead, she strapped on her boots and headed to the country for a walk. She needed the exercise to clear her mind.

Tomorrow was Saturday, Finn had said that they would make decisions then. What decisions? In the past, whenever there had been trouble, whenever life had become difficult, she had just moved on. There had been no need to work out solutions to problems. Just leave them behind.

Now this was a problem she couldn't move away from. And as she walked it became more and more clear exactly what the problem was. It wasn't Eleanor. Eleanor was now part of— no, practically the whole of—her life. The problem was Finn. What was she to do about him? How could they share Eleanor? And there was another problem. The distance between her and Finn was diminishing. The evil days of their arguing seemed vaguer now. And there seemed to be a tentative attraction growing between them. Or an old attraction reasserting itself.

That evening Eleanor was looking forward to the weekend. Just before she crawled into the Wendy house she asked Alanna, 'Do you like riding horses?'

'I love riding horses. I've ridden a lot. Shall I give you a horse ride now?'

'On your head? Like Daddy does?'

'Not quite. I'll sit here and you can sit on my knee and I'll bounce you up and down.'

'Bouncy-bouncy,' Eleanor shouted. 'I'm on Auntie Alanna horse going bouncy-bouncy.'

It was so good to hold that warm little body. Even if Eleanor was a rather enthusiastic rider.

Finn came in as they were playing and smiled at them. 'Auntie Alanna is a horse and she likes riding horses,' Eleanor told him. 'Can we go riding with Jane tomorrow morning, Daddy? And can Auntie Alanna ride? She's ridden a lot.'

This came as a bit of a surprise to Finn. He frowned at Alanna. 'Would you like to go riding?' he asked.

'I'd like to go anywhere where Eleanor wants to go,' Alanna said, slipping her daughter off her knee. 'If she wants to go riding, fine. But I'll just watch.'

She noted that Finn's voice was carefully neutral. 'I've got a…friend called Jane Lascelles who runs a riding school. She's divorced, has a teenage daughter who's at boarding school. I treated the daughter at Easter, her mother was unnecessarily grateful and invited Eleanor up to ride on a Shetland pony called Daisy.'

'I love Daisy!' a voice came from inside the Wendy house.

'So you go up there a lot? You've become friends?'

'Eleanor loves to ride on Daisy. And I like Jane.' Alanna thought that Finn's voice was firmly non-committal. Was there something he wasn't telling her? Still, could she object if there was?

In fact Alanna liked Jane at once. Finn introduced her as a friend he had known for years who had just come back to Benthwaite. There was a firm handshake and then the little group walked down to the stables. For a moment Alanna looked longingly at the horses in their boxes, but then they were led across the yard to the paddock. Daisy was waiting, already saddled. Eleanor ran across to her, gave her a pat.

There was a small black riding hat for Eleanor and then she was lifted onto Daisy and walked around the paddock. After a couple of circuits, Jane took the bridle and made Daisy trot—there were squeals of excitement and joy from Eleanor.

Finn and Alanna leaned on the paddock fence, watching their daughter. 'Have you done much riding?' he asked her.

'Here and there. No so much as a sport, rather as a means of getting from one place to another.'

'You seem to have led an exciting life since we parted.'

'I would have swapped it at once for a boring job and having a daughter. You did better than me, Finn.'

'True.' He looked across the paddock, and then said, 'Sorry if I seem a bit irritable.'

'You said it. We both have to make…make adjustments.'

'Adjustments.' He thought a minute. 'Now, that's a good word for it.'

Eventually Jane decided that Eleanor had had enough. Eleanor didn't agree but was persuaded to get down with the promise of orange juice with ice.

The four of them sat in Jane's lounge, orange juice for Eleanor, tea for the three adults.

'So are you back for good or is this a flying visit?' Jane asked Alanna.

Alanna saw Finn glance at her but he said nothing. 'I haven't made any definite plans yet,' she said. 'But I shall probably be staying for a while.'

Jane smiled. 'Next time you come up I'll have a horse saddled. Eleanor says you like to ride and I saw the way you were looking at the horses.'

'Just looking. But I used to ride a lot.'

'Well, the offer is there if you want to take it up.'

Finn stood. 'I think we've taken enough of your time, Jane. We'd better be on our way. And I can see a car coming up the track. You've got customers.'

'Well, come back whenever you can. Eleanor's practically the only person who rides Daisy. And you come, too, Alanna.'

'I'd like to,' said Alanna.

Driving on the way back home with Eleanor asleep in the back seat, well aware that her elaborately casual tone was not fooling him for a minute, Alanna said, 'Jane seems very nice. She seems fond of Eleanor—and you.'

'She is, and I like her a lot.'

Alanna waited for him to add to this, but he

didn't. So she went on, 'But you aren't…that is, you haven't…'

His voice was stern. 'Jane has been badly hurt once. She would be a fine wife and she is a fine mother. What she needs is the offer of permanence and commitment—not a quick, casual affair.' He paused a moment and then said in a quieter voice, 'I can guess what she's vaguely thought about me. That we would be well suited. But I've tried to indicate to her that there's no future for us except friendship.' He paused a moment longer and said, 'Besides, I'm still married. In fact, we're still married. Aren't we?'

It came as a shock to Alanna to hear him say that, but she said, 'Well, yes. I suppose we are. I thought you might have divorced me—if you can without the other person being informed. I just don't know. Why didn't you try, Finn?'

He was a while in replying, then said, 'I never felt the need. Never found anyone else I wanted to marry.'

'I'm glad you didn't divorce me,' she said. 'Apart from anything else, it makes dealing with Eleanor easier.'

'Anything else? What else?'

She didn't know what else. 'Just mumbling,' she said.

They went back to his house for lunch. She had noticed with some surprise what a good cook he had turned into, and felt just a bit inadequate. 'Would you like me to make lunch?' she asked.

She grinned as she saw him hesitate before he said yes. 'I am quite competent, you know,' she said, 'competent at certain things. Remember how I used to make scrambled eggs? I'd cut up all the leftover bits in the fridge, fry them up then drop the eggs on top of the mixture and…'

'I remember very well.' he said, and the coldness in his voice jerked her back to reality.

For a moment it had been a golden memory. But then she remembered how once she had cooked that very meal for him. He had come in late—very late—after a hard day in the department and told her he'd had something to eat on the way home. He hadn't bothered to phone and tell her. In a fit of temper she had taken the frying-pan and thrown its contents straight into the bin. Of course, both of them had been madly

busy, she'd had a hard day herself, and...
Memories were treacherous.

So she raided his fridge and, instead of scrambled eggs, made a quick ham salad. Eleanor loved salad. Which pleased Alanna no end.

'I thought we might go to the seaside this afternoon,' he suggested after they had finished lunch. 'It's only twenty-five miles away and Eleanor loves the waves. We can take buckets and spades and the rest of the gear and have a beach picnic. And as it's so warm, we could take our bathing costumes. Even if we can't swim, we can paddle and sunbathe a bit.'

'Sounds a great plan. You get Eleanor ready and I'll knock up a few sandwiches.'

They were on their way twenty minutes later. He took her to the lonely west coast, a forgotten bit of Lakeland, where they could park right by the beach. She changed in the car while he took Eleanor and their things to the beach little camp.

Then, just a bit nervous in her very revealing white bikini, she walked to the sands. She saw the flicker of appreciation in his eyes as he looked at her.

He had erected a windbreak and got out a couple of deckchairs. He handed Alanna a bottle of sunblock to slather all over Eleanor. 'Sticky!' shouted Eleanor. 'Sticky!'

'I'll go and change myself now,' he said, grinning, 'then will you cover me with oil with equal enthusiasm?'

Alanna was now rubbing the cream into her own legs. 'I would if you were four,' she said, 'but I think you're probably old enough to do it yourself now.'

'True. I'm grown-up, I've learned to look after myself.'

Was there a little barb in that comment? Alanna wondered as he walked back towards the car. Possibly. She shrugged. It didn't really matter.

He returned wearing shorts, his shirt hung over his shoulders. He dropped the shirt on a deckchair as Alanna handed him the sunblock. As he bent to rub his legs Alanna looked at his body. It had altered since she'd last seen it. He had been lean, wiry, now he had filled out a little. He was more muscular but there was still no touch of fat. It was a body to make any woman's heart beat. She had to own up to it, it made her heart beat. More than just a little.

She looked away as he stood to apply cream to his arms and chest. 'Turn round,' he said.

'What?'

'I see you've covered most of yourself with sunblock. But no way can you reach your back. I'll do it for you.'

'No, there's no need.' She hadn't expected this, was unprepared. It was a reasonable thing to say, she knew—it was even kind. But it would mean him putting his hands on her body and for some reason the thought worried her.

His voice was patient. 'I'm afraid there is a need. Every summer we get cases in the hospital of people who just aren't aware how dangerous the sun can be. Most we treat and send away to be uncomfortable, a few are admitted. Now, let me do your back.'

'I suppose you're right.' She turned, felt the coolness of the sunblock on her skin, felt his fingers gently massaging it in. She tried to tell herself that this was just a friend helping her. But her body told her otherwise. She was reacting to his touch.

He was quickly finished and she tried to ignore the thought that it would have been nice if he'd gone on a little longer. 'Now it's your turn to do my back,' he said.

Fair enough. She'd worked out that this would come next, she was prepared. But when she put her hands on the muscles of his warm back it was impossible not to feel an illicit pleasure.

This is my estranged husband, she told herself angrily. We were married, we parted because we couldn't stand each other. Don't forget that.

He didn't seem aware of any of the conflicting emotions swirling around her mind. Instead, when she had finished he stretched himself out on one of the deckchairs and picked up a newspaper. 'This is a day of rest for me,' he said. 'You can be the put-upon mother. Why not go for a paddle?'

'I want to paddle,' shouted Eleanor, catching the word. 'Want to paddle in the sea.'

'Right,' said Alanna, and stretched out her

hand to her daughter. 'Eleanor, let's go and paddle.' Hand in hand they ran down to the sea.

The water was still chilly but Eleanor revelled in it. She didn't mind being splashed, she loved splashing Alanna. She laughed and screamed and sat in the water with her feet in the air. She told Alanna that she was learning to swim in the pool at the big school but the sea was different. She liked them both.

The sun was warm, the breeze calm, and after a while the water seemed less cold. In the distance Alanna could see the low hills of Scotland at the other side of the Solway Firth. She was with her daughter and she was happy. What of the future? It didn't matter. She had now.

Eventually Eleanor thought they had paddled enough. They walked back up the beach, Alanna took a towel hanging on the windbreak and wrapped it around her daughter's little body.

'Daddy's asleep,' Eleanor whispered. 'Mus' keep quiet.' He was stretched out in his deck-chair, the newspaper over his head. But his body was visible, clad only in those shorts. Once again Alanna felt excitement at the sight of it, once again she thrust the thought down. It was just a normal female reaction to a male body, she assured herself.

Eleanor keeping quiet seemed to make more noise than Eleanor being her normal self, and Finn soon woke. Probably he'd only been dozing. 'Had a good paddle, you two?' he asked drowsily. 'I've had a good sleep. What shall we do now?'

'Throw the ball,' said Eleanor.

So they stood on the sand and threw the ball to each other. Sometimes they caught it, sometimes not and there was an awful lot of running around. Then there was a sandcastle to be made and after that the sandwiches to be eaten. And the weather stayed as bright as ever. It was a golden afternoon.

But Eleanor was only a little girl and eventually she tired and didn't want to play any more. 'She'll get a bit awkward in a couple of minutes,' Finn told Alanna. 'Perhaps we'd better call it a day.' So they loaded the car with the picnic equipment and set off for home. Alanna sat in the back with Eleanor and tried to keep her awake. It would be better if she didn't sleep quite yet.

Once home Alanna bathed the little girl while Finn fixed her a quick meal. They worked like a team, like two parents, Alanna thought. They were two parents! But they weren't exactly a team.

Then it was teeth-cleaning time, and story time, which Alanna did. Finn was cooking. But Eleanor's eyes closed before the story was even half-over. Alanna kissed her daughter on the forehead. She'd had a good day.

Alanna had a shower herself and then put on a dress that she had ironed earlier. She only possessed a couple of dresses, this was the better of the two. But for once she wanted to look attractive. She took more care with her hair, used a little make-up. Then she surveyed herself in the mirror. Though she said it herself, she didn't look too bad. The pink of the dress contrasted well with her tanned skin. It was almost sleeveless, the front fairly low. She looked feminine.

She needed to look her best, it would give her confidence. She may look feminine but that didn't mean that she wasn't able to fight. If need be.

This evening she had Finn were going to have

a talk. There were hard decisions to be made. She didn't know whether they would have a discussion, a negotiation or a fight. In the past it had always ended as a fight. Unfortunately there was now more to fight for. She sighed. She wished she could look forward to what was to come.

Their past record wasn't good. After the death—they'd thought then—of their child, they had been unable to give way to each other. They had both seemed to have retreated into a selfishness in which they were completely unable to recognise the other's point of view. Perhaps this evening would be different. She hoped so.

When she went downstairs she found that he apparently felt the same way as she did. Their meal was not to be in the comfortable kitchen but in the small dining room—they hadn't used it so far. He too had changed into something almost formal, a white shirt and dark trousers.

They looked at each other in silence for a moment and then he said, 'You look very…well.'

'Thank you. And you look very smart.'

Looking well and looking smart, she thought. What a couple of compliments.

He offered her a sherry. She didn't often drink it but on occasions it was quite nice. And this meal was going to be an occasion. It was going to be something to remember. But for what reasons she was still not sure.

The dining-room table was set out formally, the cutlery was silver, there were three glasses to each place setting, the napkins were linen. And she knew the food would be worthy of the setting.

'How did you become such a good cook?' she asked. 'As I remember, we used to live on take-aways and toast.'

He thought for a moment. 'I learned to live more slowly. To enjoy and appreciate the good things in life. So I taught myself to cook and I enjoy it.' He sipped his sherry. 'What was your food like abroad? Was there anything exciting and exotic?'

'Not really. I ate a lot of local food because that was all there was.'

He nodded. 'What was the most exciting place you visited?'

It seemed like a courteous exchange between two old friends, and she supposed that was what it was. But there was always the prospect of what was to come. But as they ate she told him something of where she had been, what had been good and what had been bad. The beauty she had found in South America, some of the degradation in Africa. He was obviously interested, she enjoyed telling him about her life.

And the meal was superb. Salad with locally smoked salmon and beautiful rolls. He told her that he baked the bread himself. There was a wonderfully rich beef in red wine stew, with fresh vegetables, again local. He told her he had made the stew in large quantities and frozen it. Then there was the customary fruit salad and local cream. Afterwards cheese and biscuits.

There was both red wine and white wine on the table. She enjoyed one glass, but decided to drink sparingly. It was important to keep a clear head. She noticed that he did the same.

When the meal was finished, she thanked him for it. Then they walked into the living room and he brought a tray with coffee and brandy. She noticed that this time he did not sit next to her on the couch. Instead, he sat opposite her in an easy chair. Perhaps a degree of opposition there. They were about to…well, she hoped negotiate. But even in negotiation there was a degree of opposition.

He poured the coffee and she watched as, as usual, he stirred in his half-spoonful of sugar a good ten times. It reminded her of… No going to the past now!

'We have to talk,' he said. 'In the past we often started off saying we had to talk and then finished by arguing. We made things worse, not better. But then there were just the two of us. We could—we did—pay for our own mistakes. Now there are the three of us and I won't have Eleanor suffer because…'

Apparently he saw that she had tensed. He stopped speaking. After a moment he said, 'Sorry. What I meant was that we must both try to ensure that her life continues to be as happy as it is today.'

'Agreed,' she said flatly. 'There's one thing, though…and I'm going to say even though it seems harsh and I don't mean it to be that way. One thing is not negotiable. She is my daughter and I'm never going to be parted from her again.'

He didn't reply. She saw he was trying to keep his temper. She went on, 'Finn, I'm not saying that because I feel I've got rights or because I feel entitled. I'm saying it because I love her. You must believe that.'

'I do believe it,' he said after a while. 'But you must also remember that she is my daughter, too. Tell me, have you any idea of taking her off on one of these foreign jaunts of yours?'

There was a simple answer. 'None. I had an offer I was probably going to take up in Peru— but I have other things to think about now. I don't think I've worked in any one place so far where I'd want to have my daughter—though this Peru job could be different.'

'Right, then. Would you think of going off and leaving her? Get itchy feet after a few months? Are you going to be able to give up the freewheeling life of the past four years?'

She started to answer and then held back. 'It will be hard,' she conceded, 'but I can do it.'

'Can you? You seem in doubt.'

Well, she was, she had to admit. 'Having a daughter, it makes a lot of difference,' she told him.

They both fell silent for a moment. Then he said, 'I've been thinking about this, Alanna. You've only said what I expected. What I might have said if our positions had been reversed. Now, you say you won't be parted from her and I have to say the same. You don't know her all that well yet. but Eleanor is still only a child. She might have been wonderful with you over the past three days but at times she can become a positive pain. You need to experience that before you make any definite decisions.'

Alanna frowned. 'I've dealt with awkward children before, Finn. Lots of them in hospital.'

'For some reason, your own child always finds out the way to irritate you the most. You can't distance yourself from her when the shift is over.'

'I'll be able to cope.' And Alanna knew this was true.

There was silence for a moment. They both seemed to feel that some kind of agreement had been reached, some new understanding, and both were relieved.

'I want your help,' she said after a while. 'This is something completely different and it's a bit sad. But I want to know how you dealt with it so perhaps I can do the same.'

'I know what you're going to ask. But ask it anyway.'

She didn't doubt that he meant what he'd said. There had been times, when they'd been closest, that they had been so attuned that they'd been able to could read each other's thoughts. She was glad that they could still do it. 'A week ago, before I came here, I went up onto the Yorkshire moors where we had scattered our baby's…the baby's…ashes. I took some flowers and threw them into the brook. Now I find that it's not my baby I've been mourning for the past four years. And I feel sort of…disloyal to that poor soul. She's got nobody.'

He nodded. 'I thought that's what might worry you. And you wonder if I felt the same and how I coped?'

'Yes. I know I should be ecstatic with happiness at finding Eleanor, and I am. But there's that lingering sadness.'

'I felt it, too. In the end I went to our local vicar—he's a friend of mine—and told him what had happened. We arranged a short memorial service for that little girl, and there's a plaque with her name—her real name, Eleanor Dawson—on it in the churchyard. I take flowers there sometimes. It brings me a surprising amount of comfort. Would you like to come with me to see it?'

'Not yet. But eventually. Finn, that was a lovely thing to do.'

'You'd have thought of something similar. Now, let's have another brandy.'

His voice had changed. They were now in decision-making mode again. He said, 'Right, then. Here's a suggestion. Let's postpone any decision about Eleanor's future, bring her up together for three months and then see how things are.'

Alanna frowned again. 'What do you mean, bring her up together? Are you suggesting that I get a cottage here and we alternate days or weeks or something?'

'No. That would only upset her—and us.' She

looked up, saw he had a half-smile on his face. 'Remember we're still technically married, Alanna. So move back in with me. Be Mrs Cavendish.'

He reached into his pocket, took out something and dropped it onto the coffee-table in front of them. It rattled as it spun and settled. 'Your wedding ring,' he said. 'I picked it up from the floor where you threw it.'

She looked at him in amazement. And suddenly there was a vast temptation. It would be so easy to pick it up, slip it on her finger and… But she reached forward to push the ring back towards him across the table. After a while she said, 'I couldn't wear it. It's Saturday. I only met you again on Wednesday. As I came down that hill into Benthwaite I just couldn't forget the misery of those last few months together. You may have changed a bit…but now are you expecting me to climb straight back into your bed?'

'No.' His voice was flat. 'Keep your bedroom. This is only a trial period for three months. Sex between us might be great but it would only cloud the issue. And the biggest issue is Eleanor's happiness.'

'There are other issues?'

'There's still you and me. We're going to have to see a lot of each other. How are we going to get on?'

'I suppose you're right,' she said. She wasn't quite sure about what he had said or what she felt. She thought for a while about his proposal and then said, 'Since we're being brutally honest with each other, there's a couple of things we have to get straight. You've told me about Jane Lascelles. But are you in any other kind of relationship at all?'

'No. There have been a couple of brief affairs but they came to nothing.' He paused a moment, then said, 'What about you? Then he added, 'You don't have to answer if you don't want to. I'll accept that.'

In fact she didn't like answering, but she felt she had to be honest. She muttered, 'Something like you. A couple of brief affairs that came to nothing.'

'So neither of us have any commitments. Do

you want some time to think about my proposal? Or have you any other suggestion to make?'

'No,' she said after a while. 'I think this is the best idea there is. In some ways it's just putting off a final decision, but you're right, it will give us time to consider. But what do we tell people and what do we tell Eleanor? I know it's foolish but I do want her to call me Mummy.'

'I can imagine. But perhaps it'll be better if we keep you as Auntie Alanna until we come to a final settlement. As to people, well, you don't want to be Mrs Cavendish, and now I think about it, it's probably a poor idea. There's a few people living here who remember we were married, but we'll ignore their questions. Let them think what they like. You'll just be a woman living with me.'

He grinned. 'It'll be a change from the normal. A lot of people live together and pretend to be married. We're doing the opposite. We're living together, married and pretending not to be.'

'Very droll,' she said.

'So it's settled. Are you going to take up Harry's offer of a job?'

'Are you going to tell him that you're happy with me to take it up?'

Another grin. 'I think so. We don't need a formal interview.'

'Then I'm actually looking forward to the job.'

He had refilled their small glasses of brandy. Now, by unspoken mutual consent, they both leaned forward to pick up their glasses.

She looked at the wedding ring on the table. 'I'm not going to wear that ring,' she said, 'but may I have it back?'

'Of course. I did give it to you.'

She picked it up. For a moment again she considered slipping it back on her finger, see how it fitted. Then she decided. Not yet. She didn't know what she was feeling. But there was something that she still felt she had to say.

'Finn, I'm glad I'm still—technically if you like—married to you. Being with you the past three days has been wonderful. Mostly, of course, it's been because of Eleanor. But quite a bit of it has been you. Just being with you.'

'I've enjoyed being with you, too,' he said.

Then both of them decided that things had gone far enough. For now.

CHAPTER SEVEN

FINN lay awake in bed that night, wondering if he had done the right thing. He had thought long and hard about it. He knew that Alanna would never now be parted from her daughter. To be honest, he admired her for it. Even though the strength of her feelings frightened him.

The three-month plan he had worked out seemed to him to be the only way out of the situation. And he knew it was a temporary solution. But the only alternative to that seemed to have been her renting a cottage somewhere and sharing Eleanor. This was not a good idea. For a start, rentable cottages weren't easy to come by. So they had to be thrown together.

He wondered if he wished that Alanna had never returned. He had been happy before. In time he felt sure that he would have found a woman he wanted to marry, a woman who would be a good mother to Eleanor. He might even have changed his mind about Jane. But Alanna was here now. She had to be dealt with.

For the first time he started thinking, not about Eleanor, Alanna and himself but about Alanna and himself. When he remembered their last few months together he screwed up his face in anguish. They had been dreadful. How could two people who had been so much in love turn on and torture each other? When she had gone he had heaved a sigh of relief. They had loved each other. But that love seemed out of reach.

He remembered something that he had once been told, a word of caution. Things once said can be forgiven but they can never be unsaid. People might forgive but they don't forget.

Could Alanna have changed? It seemed a possibility. But one thing was certain, no way could he have Eleanor in the middle of the rows he remembered so well.

He had been tired, had had a good day. But now his thoughts had made him wide awake. He turned restlessly in his bed. Those days just couldn't come back!

But what about the past four days? They had been fraught for both Alanna and himself. But as he thought about them, he realised he had very much enjoyed them. And Eleanor already doted on…on her mother. Just for a moment he felt a pang of jealousy. He and Eleanor had been all right before. Why should things change now? Why should he have to share her?

More thoughts!

Yes, he had quite enjoyed the past four days. There were moments in Alanna's company when the evil memories disappeared and he re-membered the many years he had known her, his delight in her company. She had changed now. But there were still echoes of the person he had once thought so wonderful.

Just before he finally fell asleep he wondered if they had a future together. And what it could be.

Alanna felt strange to be dressed as a British nurse and working again in a British hospital. There were resources, the knowledge that they would never run out of equipment or medicine. There was always a helping hand somewhere if it was needed. No more did she find herself making life and death decisions which she was not trained or equipped to make. But it was still hard work.

Rosewood sent its most serious cases to the big hospital at Carlisle. But it had the resources for minor surgery and also a twenty-four-hour A and E department. Once again it could only handle the more minor casualty cases—in fact, nurses dealt with most of them. But most A and E admission were for minor things.

It was a great, a much-loved resource for the local people. And when some bigwig in London had thought that it ought to close for financial reasons, there had been a howl of rage from the townspeople.

Technically, she was working as a practice nurse for Harry. But as so much of the practice work took place in the hospital, she would spend much of her time there. It was an apparently casual system, but it worked well.

On Monday morning she had been doing some washing in Finn's house when her mobile phone rang. It was Finn, one of the few people to have the number. She worried at once. 'What is it, Finn? Is Eleanor all right?'

His voice was ironic. 'I think so. I last saw her an hour ago when she was learning to sing. No, Alanna, it's you I want. Remember sometimes you used to help me in Theatre? Have you kept up those skills?'

An odd question. she thought, but still… 'I've kept up my skills. I've even done a little minor surgery myself. But not the kind of theatre work you'd recognise. Poor equipment, sometimes even done out of doors. Why?'

'I've got a list of minor surgery here. The part-time anaesthetist has turned up but my usual scrub nurse is ill. So do you want to come to save the day? I've phoned Harry and he's seeing to your insurance and so on.'

Her heart beat a little faster at the prospect of working with Finn again. 'Finn, I'd love to.'

'Can you be here in an hour?'

'I'm on my way.'

She had forgotten just how competent Finn was. Recently she had seen a new Finn, relaxed, easygoing. This was the old Finn, aware of nothing but the job in front of him.

But perhaps that wasn't exactly true. In Leeds, even when they had been happily married and working in Theatre together, he had never referred to her as anything but Nurse. Now he called her Alanna. As he called the anaesthetist Jack.

She enjoyed the morning's work. The procedures were only minor, an ingrowing toenail to be removed and a varicose vein stripped. But they took precision and skill on the part of both doctor and nurse. They'd always worked well together, she'd been able to anticipate his wants even before he'd known them himself. And now they were working together again and after the initial hesitation were as slick a team as they had ever been.

'A good morning's work,' he told her as they pulled off their scrubs. 'Did you enjoy it?'

'You know I did. It all came back very quickly.'

'Good. Now, there's a message from Harry. Will you go down to the surgery to sign documents and so on? He wants you officially working for him as quickly as possible. If you like, I'll pick you up there when the day's over.'

'Sounds a good plan,' she said.

'We're old friends,' Harry said, 'but for the first few minutes I want to be formal, tell you the things I have to tell you, listen to you while you answer my questions. Then you can sign the forms and you'll be registered as a temporary practice nurse.'

'No trouble to that.'

So they finished the official business and then could talk as friends. 'I'm not entitled to ask you this as an employer,' Harry said, 'but I can as a friend. What's the situation between you and Finn and Eleanor?'

'I've just signed a three-month contract with you. And I've made an agreement with Finn. I'm going to live in the house, be Eleanor's auntie. We'll share her, I suppose. At the end of three months we'll consider what to do next. It'll give us time to breathe. Give me time to really get to know my daughter.'

'I think that's an excellent idea,' said Harry.

She looked at him, her expression mocking. 'Harry, I know what you're thinking. But don't count on it happening. I doubt we'll get together again. I'm staying at his house—but I've got my own bedroom and I'm staying in it.'

'You doubt you'll get together again. But it's still a possibility?'

It took a while before she could answer. 'Everything's possible. Things might change.' She thought a moment longer and then went on, 'Harry, we've changed. We're different people from who we were. We don't really know each other any more. Sometimes I feel that we're just…just groping for what we had.'

'Whatever,' Harry said, waving a careless hand. 'The most important thing is that now I've got a practice nurse I can rely on. Incidentally, Alanna, you've accepted the job for three months but you know there'll always be work here if you want it.'

'That's good to know,' she said.

She had made her mind up about certain things when she met Finn and Eleanor that evening.

The evening progressed much as usual. She had her usual meal with Eleanor in the Wendy House then a meal with Finn and together they put their daughter to bed. And then it was time to talk.

'I'm not going to stay here for three months as your guest,' she told Finn, 'though I have to say that I'm really truly grateful for the invitation. But I want to be involved in everything. I want to do my share of the cooking, my share of the cleaning. I want to be with you when you make any decisions about Eleanor's future, I want to buy some of her clothes without consulting you and sometimes I want to take her out by myself. All right so far?'

'Well, I can see where you're coming from,' he said, 'but carry on.'

'I'm now earning and I have some money saved up. I don't like free loading. I want to contribute to the overall costs of running the house.'

She could see that he didn't much like that. But he thought for a minute and then said, 'You must do what you want. But I thought I'd got things pretty well organised already. Eleanor seems to be happy with things.'

'Finn, I think you've done a fantastic job. You've been both mother and father to Eleanor, and done both jobs really well. But now the two jobs are separate. We're a partnership, you've got to let me in.'

'I suppose it makes sense,' he said. 'Though I was happy with things as they were before. But I don't want to take money from you.'

'Finn, you've got to take something from me! If you want I'll be very happy for you to put it into a savings account for Eleanor or something. But I pay for my share and half of Eleanor's. I need to.'

There was silence for quite a while. She managed to keep a pleasant expression on her face but it was an effort. She remembered how in the past his silences had made her want to scream. He would just refuse to discuss things. Were they going back to that?

But then he spoke. 'All right,' he said, 'I suppose it makes sense so we'll do as you say. But it makes me feel that I'm losing something.'

'I can sympathise with that,' she told him. 'Believe it or not, I can. But can't you see that you might be gaining something, too? We're a partnership—again.'

There was another, longer pause. And then he smiled and said, 'You know, I think you're right.

Slowly, Alana got used to having a daughter. She was still happier than she had ever been, but she was now becoming aware that having a child was sometimes a mixed delight.

On Wednesday evening Eleanor was a definite pain. Perhaps something was upsetting her but neither Finn nor Alanna could work out what. She was awkward, rebellious, screamed and cried at the smallest thing. She wouldn't go to bed and then wouldn't go to sleep. When Alanna finally crept downstairs, two hours later than usual, she was happy to sit next to Finn and to accept a glass of malt whisky from him.

'It's not all good times, having kids.' He grinned at her.

'I know what they're like, I've worked with children before. But if possible I tried to avoid it.'

'Why did you try to avoid it?'

'You know. Being with young children who

were likely to die made me…made me over-emotional.'

'I can imagine that.'

She thought she could detect genuine sympathy in his voice and wasn't surprised when he promptly changed the subject. 'So how do you find having a daughter now?'

'I love it! I really really love it!'

'Even after tonight's performance?'

'Perhaps tonight is part of it. When I first saw her, and knew that she was my daughter, it seemed like some kind of magic happening. Suddenly I'd had a gift from God. But now she's changing. She's not just my daughter, a bit of me—she's Eleanor, a little person, someone with a character of her own. And so I'm learning to love her in a different way.'

'Love is odd, isn't it? We loved each other, and then we destroyed it. And it was both our faults.'

'We should have known better. But, still, what's past is done.'

They sat there in silence and she realised that Finn's words had upset her more than she'd realised at first. *We loved each other, and then we destroyed it*. Well, it was true. But it now seemed to hurt more than before. And her own words. *What's past is done*. Perhaps it was—but perhaps it could be undone?

Somehow Finn seemed to catch the drift of her thoughts. 'I had to call on a patient in Roscoe Drive this morning,' he said. 'And I passed the house where you used to live with your Auntie Gladys. And then for some reason I drove round to see where I used to live with Uncle Frank in Tilson Crescent.'

'Memories,' she said. 'Were they happy?'

He sipped his whisky before answering her. 'They weren't unhappy. It was odd, the way that we were both brought up the same way. Both sets of parents dead so that we were handed on to older relatives. I know both of them tried. But they never had any real idea about how to bring up children. I'm sure they loved us in their way but they just couldn't show it. Perhaps that's what made us...how we were—perhaps how we are.'

Alanna had been tired, looking forward to relaxing after a hard if pleasant day. But now suddenly she was alert, feeling that together they might fumble towards some truth that had so far escaped them.

'Harry said that you were the best father he knew,' she said. 'It's obvious how much you love Eleanor, you show it to her every minute. And, Finn, I want to be just as good a mother. But that isn't the point just now. Do you feel that in some way that you're…you're compensating for the love you felt you didn't have as a child?'

He shook his head, as if trying to clear it. 'Not compensating, that's the wrong word. I'm just trying to make things different for her. Make her feel that, whatever happens, there's a love she can rely on unconditionally. Make her feel that there's always someone there for her. Do you know what I'm talking about?'

'I think I feel the same way,' she said slowly. 'Finn, when we were very young, we were both loners, weren't we? We relied on ourselves, we couldn't give easily. And we learned that from our guardians.'

'And then I met you,' he said with a smile. 'I mean, really met you. Though it took a long time. We were both nervous, both scared, both accustomed to keeping our feelings in check. But at long last there was someone whose hand I could hold, someone I could rely on, who I could be happy with just because they were there. Those were golden days, Alanna.'

'You had someone who loved you,' she said gently. 'And I did, and I knew you loved me. So what went wrong?'

'Early experience goes deep. My escape from worry had always been to work. Your escape had been to move on. So when things got too much for us—we both retreated. Became self-absorbed, unable to reach out even if we wanted to.'

'Are we like that now?'

'I think it's still in us. The past four or five years prove that.'

'And the love that we had?'

'I think that's probably still in us, too. Time will tell.'

Alanna finished her drink, leaned towards him and kissed him on the cheek. 'I'm glad we've talked,' she said, 'but now I've got a lot to think about so I'm going to bed.'

He caught her arms as she made to move away from him, pulled her towards him and gently kissed her—also on the cheek. 'Goodnight, Alanna,' he said.

She had a good week. Sometimes she worked in the cottage hospital, other times she worked in the surgery. Once or twice she made home visits. Finn happily lent her his Land Rover. She was meeting new people, renewing her acquaintance with others. She could tell that everyone she met was curious about her relationship with Finn but so far no one had actually asked her to explain. So she said nothing. Things would work out in the end.

In the middle of her third week in Benthwaite she asked Finn if he would take her to the railway station in Carlisle on the following Saturday morning.

Both of them had Saturday off but would be working on Sunday. There was a complex system of organising the staff rota, because there had to be a presence at the hospital over every weekend. The system worked because everyone was willing to make allowances.

'I'll happily take you,' said Finn. 'Where are you going?'

'I've got some trunks full of personal stuff stored at SAMS in Leeds,' she told him. 'That's the charity I've worked for occasionally. Their headquarters are in Leeds. As I'm staying here a while longer, I'd like to fetch a few things.'

'Going by train would be foolish. Why don't you take the Land Rover? It would be easier. Or, even better, would you like Eleanor and I to go with you? We could share the driving.'

She hesitated. 'Why would you want to come with me?'

'Eleanor likes car rides and I haven't been to Leeds for a while.' He looked at her thoughtfully and went on, 'And there's a couple of places I need to visit.'

So it was decided. They set off early Saturday morning, Eleanor as usual pleased to be moving. Alanna felt a bit strange and wondered how Finn felt. But he seemed in a good mood. She remembered past occasions when they had left Benthwaite for Leeds—how they had been looking forward to a new good life. Now they were visiting the scene of an old bad one.

'Looking forward to seeing Leeds again?' she asked.

'Sort of. You never know how journeys will end, do you? You're just at the start.'

'Very philosophical,' she said.

As they drove, they played travelling games with Eleanor. Alanna really enjoyed them. There was so much pleasure being with her child—so many different kinds of pleasure. She felt angry that she had not been able to enjoy them all from the beginning.

She had wanted to breast-feed her child and had never been able to. So many times she had seen that expression of drowsy contentment in the eyes of breast-feeding women, and she had envied it.

She closed her eyes then opened them, and saw Finn glance over at her.

'Are you OK?' he asked softly.

Face up to things, it was her way. Quietly she said, 'I was thinking that I never breast-fed Eleanor, and I was feeling sorry for myself.'

'You still might get to breast-feed a child,' he

said. 'You're young, there's years of child-bearing in you.'

'Yes, I suppose so, but I...' she started, and then decided to say nothing more. She didn't want to talk to Finn about the possibility of her having children. 'Look, Eleanor, see that bird! It's just staying still in the air.'

'Bird in the air,' said Eleanor.

The three of them were allowed into the store-room at SAMS where her trunks were stored. Casually, she asked if Gabriel was there, then was happy when she was told that he was away at a conference in London. She didn't want to meet him. He was a reminder of a different life.

She had just three trunks stored. When she had parted from Finn she had systematically got rid of everything that might remind her of her previous life. She had sold, given away, de-stroyed—anything to sweep away the memories. Books, clothes, CDs, pictures, all had gone. Afterwards she had felt freer, cleansed. But now she was rather regretting it all.

'This is all my life,' she said to Finn. 'It doesn't seem much, does it, compared with yours?'

'You have memories. They are much more valuable. And there are people abroad who will think of you as the woman who cured them, or cared for them. That must mean something to you.'

'It does,' she said. Then decided to change the subject. 'I'll just look through these and take a few—'

'We have the car downstairs. We could take all three trunks, if you want.'

She was tempted a moment and then decided against it. Taking everything away from here would be a step too far. This place was a link to her previous wandering life. While she had stuff here there was always an escape route again. Not that she would ever again leave Eleanor.

In the end she decided to take just one trunk. Quickly she sorted through the other two. There were a few papers—nursing certificates and so on. There were a lot of clothes—some of them a bit dated. A lot of outdoor gear. A couple of dresses, a couple of skirts and tops, some underwear. A few well remembered books. A few pictures, mementoes of places she had lived.

As she sorted she found she was becoming angry. Much of this she had hardly looked at since she had parted from Finn. And painful memories were surfacing, old wounds being reopened. Then at the bottom of one drink she came to a tightly wrapped parcel and her hands shook as she reached for it. She realised that she had known it was there but some part of her mind had stopped her thinking about it.

She should have given it away. But she hadn't been able to. Just this one parcel. With trembling fingers she tore at the wrapping. And there it was. A silk christening robe. She touched it, felt its softness. Then she looked up at Finn and suddenly her anger disappeared.

He remembered too and he knew what she was feeling. He lifted her from her position bent over the trunk, held her by the shoulders and kissed her on the cheek. 'We didn't know,' he said.

'Why are you kissing Auntie Alanna?' Eleanor asked in an interested voice and he let her go at once.

There was no way that she would ever need it, but Alanna put the christening robe in the pile of things she wanted to take.

Just one trunk to carry back. It was still quite early so they had much of the day left in front of them. 'Where do you need to visit?' she asked.

'It's a little surprise,' he said, 'I hope you don't find it too…'

'Too what?'

'Do you mind if we just wait and see?'

The left the city centre and drove off into suburbs that she remembered. Then she became uneasy. 'Finn, where are you taking me? Where are we going?' Then she realised and her voice sharpened. 'Finn, I don't want to do this! Turn around!'

He said, 'Don't shout. You'll disturb our daughter.'

Our daughter. She realised it was the first time he had ever used that phrase. Our daughter. And because he had used it, she said nothing more.

They came to a pleasant side road in a pleasant suburb. Alanna concentrated on talking to Eleanor and tried not to look out of the window.

But when he stopped the car she had to. A small, quite unremarkable block of flats. One on the first floor. On the left corner. Now with fashionable steel blinds, not gay cotton curtains.

'Selkirk Drive,' he said. 'Where we lived together for eighteen months.'

'The last nine of which were the worst months of my life,' she said. 'Largely because of you.' Then she reconsidered. 'So I thought then. I feel differently now.'

'So are you feeling angry now?'

'I can feel the emotions, I can feel them welling up again. I can feel the anger and the despair and the—I've got to say it, Finn—hatred.'

He started the car and drove on a little further. She was feeling more and more angry, remembering the rows, the screaming matches, the way he'd kept silent when she'd wanted attention, knowing he was angering her. And she thought she could stand it no longer.

'Finn, stop the car! I want to get out.'

'You can't get out. Your daughter needs you.'

'That's blackmail!'

'No, it's not. It's a careful statement of a

fact. You're a mother now, Alanna. That carries responsibilities.'

So she didn't get out. But when she saw where he was stopping the car, her anger doubled. 'Pelham Park! I don't want to stop here.'

'I thought we might walk to the fountain. Give Eleanor a run on the grass.'

'Of all the places in the world I have been, this park is the last place I want to revisit. And the fountain in the park is the worst bit of the park.'

'I think you ought to come and see it,' he said. His voice sounded strained and she realised that this wasn't easy for him. 'And if you're interested, I'm finding this as hard as you are. By that fountain we had our last, biggest row. You called me an unthinking, unfeeling work-obsessed machine. I said you just couldn't face up to life and all you wanted to do was run away. I was called out that night. When I came back next morning you were gone. I knew I could probably have found you then but I didn't want to look. Now, let's go and see that fountain!'

'Why? So we can have the same fight again?'

'No. Because we've got to put the past behind

us. We're two different people now, we need a new start. We remember the past and then decide we can go on.'

'Go on where?' She was still angry.

'Alanna, we have to do some things together, for Eleanor's sake. Perhaps for our sakes too. Now, come on, we'll each hold one of her hands and we'll walk to the fountain.'

So they did. Eleanor was entirely happy, she'd missed most of the argument which had been carried on in muttered undertones. And she loved walking between two adults, holding their hands, it meant she could swing.

After a while they reached the fountain. They stood and looked. It was dirty, there were old tins floating in the small pool, the statuary was chipped and had been daubed with paint. 'Ugly, isn't it?' she asked after a minute.

'I've never noticed before—but yes. What exactly were we arguing about?'

She considered. 'I can remember the anger, the insults. But as I look back, the argument wasn't about anything very much.'

'I think you're right.' His voice was desolate.

She could feel the anger slipping away now, leaving only sadness. 'Why did you bring me here?'

'I wanted to get over the ill feelings, try and put them behind us. We've got to see what has happened since, put the past in context. Now perhaps we can look forward—we have to, for Eleanor's sake.' He paused, and said, 'Though there might be other reasons.'

She wondered what the other reasons might be, then shied away from the thought. 'You're different,' she said. 'You wouldn't have done this four years ago. You know people so much better.'

'We both suffered,' he said. 'We dealt with it different ways.'

They walked back to the car. 'There's a fish and chip shop round the corner,' Alanna said, 'I remember being happy there.'

'Fish and chips,' shouted Eleanor. 'I want fish and chips.'

'She loves them,' said Finn.

The café hadn't changed much in the past four years—there were plastic tables and chairs and a wonderful overriding smell. The menu hadn't changed either, it was still good. All three enjoyed their meal. Eleanor had a pool of tomato sauce and dipped each chip and fish finger in it, very carefully. Well, as carefully as she could. Alanna was happy about that. It gave her an excuse. Tissues in hand, she could pretend that she was concentrating on keeping Eleanor clean.

And she and Finn exchanged the occasional comment on what they had discussed here, how tired they'd both so often been. They didn't talk too much and both were happy with the silence. Too much had been felt. They needed a rest, to relax.

And then there was the early afternoon drive back. Alanna felt exhausted but she offered to drive anyway. 'You must feel as tired as me,' she said.

'I probably do. But I'm OK to drive. I see Eleanor has gone to sleep. Why don't you do the same?' So she did. It had been an exhausting day.

After a while she woke up when there was a change in the engine note. Without him noticing, she looked in the rear-view mirror. He was studying her again. She couldn't make out what his feelings were.

The ride suddenly became much bumpier. She looked out of the window and frowned. 'Where are we going? Oh. Here, Finn?' She knew her voice registered her shock. Now she knew where they were going.

'We've just been to where we were at our worst,' he said. 'I thought we might try to capture the other bit, come back to where we were at our best. Recognise the place?'

'Oh, yes. I've never forgotten it.'

'Neither have I,' he said.

They were about six miles from Benthwaite on a lonely bit of the fell. In fact, they had cycled there. So many years ago, it seemed, while they had both still been at school. They had pushed their bikes up this track, each wondering…

The vehicle bumped up a bit further and then he swung off into a disused quarry and stopped. Eleanor woke up, a bit grizzly at first. Alanna calmed her, gave her a drink and she was soon in a good mood again.

'Are we going for a walk around?' Alanna asked.

'I thought we might. If you wanted to.'

They looked round at the rocky walls, the piles of stones. There was little recent sign of man. 'So let's see what we can find,' Alanna said.

They followed an ill-defined path, Alanna taking charge of Eleanor. At the far end of the quarry they scrambled up the slope, found a tiny patch of grass sheltered on all sides by white limestone. They stood and looked. 'Here,' she said, 'it was here.'

He sat on a boulder, watched Eleanor as she explored, completely engrossed in her surroundings. 'It was here,' he agreed.

Alanna sat opposite him, her thoughts spiralling back to the past. 'It was warm, warmer than it is today, and it was the end of summer. You were going to university to study medicine, I was going abroad on a supposed gap year. You asked me to stay and you said you loved me. And I said that I loved you, too.'

He nodded his head. 'It was the first time we ever used the word love to each other. Though I know we both felt it. Perhaps we had more sense then. But we were just children, Alanna.'

'We knew what we wanted, though,' she said, and blushed at the memory. 'You'd brought a space blanket for us to lie on.' She lowered her voice, even though Eleanor was not paying any attention to them. 'And you'd bought some… some condoms.'

He grinned. 'I had to go to Carlisle to get them. No way could I buy them locally. Everyone would have known in the next half-hour.'

The sat silent a while, each content with memories, watching their daughter. 'Why did you bring me here?' she asked eventually.

'I wanted to visit two places. The place where perhaps we'd been most unhappy and the place where perhaps we'd been happiest. Sort of brackets of our life together.'

Another few moments silence. Then, 'we were happy,' she said. 'I loved you—but I thought the first time might be…well, all the stories from the girls in school…but, in fact, it was marvellous.'

'Yes, it was.'

It was an odd way he was looking at her. She felt both uncomfortable and as if there was something that she was missing. In the end, she stood and walked over to him. Leaning over Eleanor, she kissed him quickly on the lips. 'That's for happy memories,' she said. 'But we're ten years older now. We might be wiser, we're certainly sadder.'

'True. We'd better go. Come on, Eleanor.'

As he stood, she said, 'Thank you for bringing me here. It was…' Her voice trailed away. It was what? She didn't know.

CHAPTER EIGHT

THEY drove back into Benthwaite and to his house. 'It's been a long and exciting day, but it's good to be home,' Alanna said.

'It certainly is. And it's getting late, so usual division of labour? You see to Eleanor, I'll start cooking.'

'Sounds a good plan.'

But as they fell into the now practiced routine, Alanna found herself wondering. She had said it was good to be home. She was thinking of this house as home, not just a place where she was staying and would in time leave. She had never thought of any of the places she had stayed as home. This wasn't her home! But it certainly felt like it.

She gave Eleanor her tea, bathed her and put

her to bed, read her a story, and only then called Finn up for his daughter's goodnight kiss.

'Dinner in half an hour,' he said, when Eleanor's eyes finally closed. 'I thought, as it's Saturday, we'd dine in a bit of style again. In the dining room.'

'I'm looking forward to it. But I've got to shower and change first.' She went to her room.

She remembered the last time they'd had dinner in the dining room. It had been a bit of an occasion, they'd had their long talk and had made difficult decisions. Was this going to be equally important? She thought not, but she would still recognise the occasion. Besides, she was getting a bit of a taste for dressing up. She'd done so little of it over the past four years!

First she showered, then tried to do a little extra with her hair. Now, what to wear? She rummaged through the trunk that Finn had carried to her bedroom, looked at half-forgotten clothes. There was some silk underwear there. It would feel different against her skin, different from the sensible cotton underwear she usually wore. She slipped it on, stood to look at herself. The sight made her feel oddly excited. Which dress? There were two in the trunk. She lifted them out and held them against her in turn.

The first, the white one, would do. But it was long and frilly, a bit excessive perhaps for what was, after all, only dinner. The second, a dark blue—well, call it a cocktail dress. She remembered buying it. It had been when things had been getting really bad with Finn and she had bought it largely to cheer herself up but also because they were supposed to be going to a formal ball. But at the last minute—the really last minute, she had already put the dress on—he had phoned to cancel. Of course, it had caused more anger between them. But he'd had a good reason, she had to accept that. There had been a fire in a block of flats, a large number of casualties, and all A and E staff had been asked to stay on or even come in. However, it had still made the situation worse.

So, a simple dark blue silk dress that stood outside fashion and looked really good on her. A timeless classic, it echoed the colour of her eyes, went well with her dark hair. She put on make-up, a quick touch at her hair, and looked again in the mirror. She was pleased. The silk clung to her body, showed that she was in good shape. Finn would be impressed.

She went downstairs. She had a sense of anticipation—but she wasn't sure what she was anticipating.

It was interesting that Finn seemed to have felt the same way as her. He had also changed and was now in a dark brown open-necked shirt and an almost white linen suit. He looked incredibly smart—the kind of man who would turn any woman's head. Alanna felt a tiny thrill of excitement. Just to see him, she told herself, it's nothing more than that. It can't be—at least, not yet.

He handed her a sherry. 'The food's all cooked, waiting on the hot plate. We can eat when we're ready.'

'A bit of a change from chips off a plastic table,' she told him.

'I enjoyed our lunch! But I thought we'd have a change.'

She tasted her sherry and decided that it was

a good one. She wasn't exactly a connoisseur, but over the past few years she had drunk some of the locally made wines. And many of them were terrible.

'You've changed into a man who likes to eat properly and with style,' she said. 'Not like the way we used to be.'

'So which do you prefer?'

'When I was travelling, in a lot of the places you just couldn't eat well, whether you wanted to or not. There was neither the food or the time. So I prefer this.'

He went to the sideboard, took something from a silver bucket. She heard a pop and then he was handing her a slender champagne flute full of a light bubbling liquid.

'Champagne?'

'Why not? Let's celebrate.'

'What are we celebrating?'

'It's been two and a half weeks since you came back into my life—perhaps a better way of putting it would be two and a half weeks since you learned you had a daughter. And now you're getting used to the idea. You're turning into a mother. And...so far...we two have managed a difficult situation with a fair amount of success. So here's to Alanna, the new mother, and also to us.'

'I'll drink to that.' They clinked glasses and drank. Alanna thought it was one of the most wonderful drinks she had ever tasted.

'To the new mother,' he said again, looking at her.

'I'll propose a different toast. To Finn, the wonderful father. What I thought he'd always be.'

They drank to that, too. Alanna looked at him, saw something deep in his eyes that she didn't quite understand. Another thrill of excitement—but still better to wait. 'I love this champagne,' she said. 'I could easily get used to it. But what's for dinner? It smells gorgeous and I'm ravenous.'

'Then we'll start.'

She loved his cooking—if only because it was a side of him that she had never seen when they'd been together previously. But there was another feeling, a determination that in future she would do more of the cooking. If necessary, he could teach her.

There was a cold soup with tiny bits of vegetable in it and a tang of herbs and spices. Then chicken breast wrapped in bacon with a sweet sauce and salad. Everything on the plate had come from a farm not more than twenty miles from them, he told her. Finally there was fruit and his home-made ice cream.

They agreed to leave the dishes till later. Taking the rest of the champagne into the living room, they sat side by side on the couch. He took off his jacket, threw it to one side.

She felt comfortable there. They could hear the occasional snuffles and grunts from the sleeping Eleanor through the baby alarm. Finn put on a CD and the soft sound of Sinatra filled the room. That was clever and thoughtful of him as both had been avid Sinatra fans when they'd been younger. She felt happy, at peace with the world.

'So how have you found things so far?' he asked.

'Like you said, I'm getting used to being a mother. I'm liking it, it's changing me. But now I think I'm getting over much of the shock. I can think of other things, I can notice other people. Memories are coming back and…most of them are happy. How are you feeling about having me back?'

He paused before replying. 'I was frightened,' he confessed. 'I knew you had the right to be a mother, knew what it would mean to you. And I wanted you to be happy. But a nasty bit of me felt that things had been better with you away. I was happy in my life with Eleanor.'

'And how do you feel now?'

'I know that Eleanor needs a mother and she's certainly happier now she's got one.'

Perhaps it was the champagne that had made her a little more reckless than she ought to have been. So she asked, 'But how am I affecting you? What do you feel about having me back in your life?'

'It's…hard to say. No, it isn't. I like it.'

She thought she was glad of that positive reply, but she still had her own feelings that had to be sorted out before she should think about his.

They had finished the champagne and he went into the kitchen to fetch coffee and brandy. As they drank, she said, 'It might be that wonderful meal, or that wonderful champagne, but I feel at ease with the world. Today has been good for me. It was brave of you to take me to those two places, to the park and to the old quarry. I feel that I've settled some of the past and now it's truly behind me. Behind us. And now I'm starting to get used to Eleanor… Like I said, I can look around a bit. I can see you, think of you. There's no…no red mist of distrust any more.'

'So what do you see?' His voice was apparently casual, but she suspected there was a lot more to the question than he tried to show.

'There's a new you that I like. You've always been a good doctor but now you're gentler, more easygoing. And now I'm remembering only the good bit of our previous life.' She paused, aware that she had to pick her words with tremendous care. 'I really loved you…then, Finn.'

The silence seemed to go on and on. Then he said, 'Loved me…then?'

'I don't really know what I'm feeling now,' she confessed. 'I'm all mixed up. How about you? What do you feel about me? Then and now. I can't sort them out myself but…when I look at you I…' She drank a little of her brandy then carefully placed the glass back on the table. 'When I look at you I just don't know.'

She lay back on the comfortable cushions of his couch, her head resting back, her hands on her lap, her eyes closed. There had been too much worrying over the past few days. She didn't want to make any decisions. She didn't want to think any more. She just wanted to be.

She felt the couch dip as Finn moved closer to her. Felt his arm around her shoulders, the pressure of the side of his thigh against hers. She felt his chest as he leaned across her. She could smell the faint touch of his after shave mixed with the warmth of his body. It was exciting. And in the background Sinatra sang…

His arm tightened. She felt, knew, that his face was approaching hers and her lips parted in anticipation. She didn't want to think. She just wanted to be. Just wanted…

It was the softest of kisses. The second before his lips touched hers there was a moment of fear, of panic even, and she tensed. She knew that he felt her involuntary movement because he hesitated. But then she relaxed, sighed softly. And stretched one arm loosely around his waist. She eased him towards her.

But it was still the gentlest of kisses, his lips only just touching hers. There was the taste of brandy, that must also be on her lips, too. It was nice. They stayed there together for a minute and although he made no movement she could feel his heart beating faster, his breath deepening with excitement.

His lips moved from her mouth, kissed her cheeks, her forehead, the tip of her chin. Then he leaned his cheek against hers, eased her head to one side, took the lobe of her ear in his mouth. Delicately, he bit. She shivered with excitement. 'You remembered,' she mumbled with excitement. 'You know what that does to me. You remembered.'

'Who could forget?' was the hoarse answer. 'You taste so sweet.'

Having him nibble her ear had always been something that delighted and excited her.

Another gentle nip and then his mouth came down on hers. Now he was more insistent, demanding. She clutched him to her as her lips gave way to his demands. He was sweet, too!

And somehow she found that they were lying side by side on the couch, he was kissing her neck, her throat, moving down the swell of her breasts above the low top of her dress.

She wanted him to kiss her there. Her nipples, painfully tight against the lace of her bra, knew that they wanted him to take them into his mouth…

'Not here,' she whispered. 'I want to do it properly. I want you to take me to bed, Finn. Don't you want to?' Her voice was ragged with emotion.

'You know I do! But, Alanna, we can stop now…just. If this isn't what you want…'

'If I wanted to stop, I shouldn't have started,' she pointed out. 'And if I wanted you to stop, I would have stopped you before now. What are we doing lying here, talking?'

'Good question.' He stood, took her hands and pulled her upright. His arms went around her for another deep long-lasting kiss that made her senses whirl. 'Last time of asking,' he said. 'We could stop now—but after this not at all.'

Now she had no hesitation. 'Come on,' she said. Her arms went around his waist, she urged him towards the stairs. It took time to get to his bedroom. It appeared that they had to kiss every second step.

She had always liked his bedroom, it was masculine but comfortable. She liked the fact that it had a large double bed with light blue cotton sheets and a dark blue pillow. They got there at last, he sat her on the edge of the bed and gave her a kiss. Then he went over to close the curtains.

While his back was turned she pulled her dress over her head, kicked off her shoes. When he turned she was standing there, a small smile on her face, dressed in nothing but scraps of white silk. She heard his breath escape as he looked at her, felt pleasure at what she was doing to him, the effect she was having on him. It made her feel both powerful and a little afraid. What had she started—or, rather, what had they started?

When he came towards her she said, 'You're a bit overdressed.' She pushed his hands away from where they were about to wrap around her, made him stand as one by one she undid the buttons of his shirt. She slid it off him, threw it on a chair. For a moment she placed both hands flat on his muscled chest, felt it rising and falling. He was breathing faster than usual.

She unbuckled his belt, slid his trousers downwards. He was wearing dark grey boxers, his need for her instantly apparent. 'Oh,' she said.

Now it was his turn. He kicked off his trousers, shoes and socks, folded her into his arms again and pressed both of their nearly naked bodies together as he kissed her. She felt her growing need for what must come next, muttered his name, tried to tell him what it was she wanted. 'Love me, Finn, love me,' she muttered. 'Love me now.'

But he was in no hurry. Clever hands unfastened her bra. He took it from her outstretched arms and then bent to take a hard-pointed breast into his mouth. His tongue rasped across her nipple, causing her to cry out in ecstasy. Then his fingers were inside the elastic of her knickers, slowly he slid them downwards and it was her turn to kick them to one side.

She was naked. What would he do now?

He bent, picked her up bodily and laid her on his bed. She marvelled at his strength, she was no anorexic waif. Then he was on the bed beside her. He captured her mouth in another long-lasting kiss that seemed to pull at her very soul.

Perhaps it could have taken longer. But it had been so long and their need for each other was so great. It seemed only seconds before he was above her… And then some distant part of her brain warned her. 'Finn…you need something,' she said. 'That is, we need something.'

He paused only long enough to snatch a quick kiss. 'I know, sweetheart,' he said. 'Just one minute.'

He rolled away from her and she heard the bedside cabinet drawer slide open, the tearing of foil. His back was turned to her but she was quite happy to wait now, hands behind her neck, knowing how she would appear to him when he turned back.

Then he—they—were ready. For a moment he leaned above her, looking down at her naked body, and she revelled at the feelings she saw in his eyes. She put up a hand to smooth it across his chest then reached down lower so he groaned with delight. And then…a moment's fear but then inside her a feeling as if he was coming home, a feeling of absolute rightness. She knew his desperation matched her own, their bodies swayed and plunged together perfectly in harmony until, so quickly, they reached final acceptance together, and it seemed as if the heavens melted and the wide world rocked beneath her.

Two warm, sweat-bathed bodies and they waited for their racing hearts to slow. But now it was cooler. He reached down, pulled a sheet over them. She wrapped her arms round his neck, pulled him to her. 'Sweetheart,' he muttered, 'I think we should—'

She laid a finger across his mouth. 'Not yet. That was so wonderful. I just want to remember and enjoy it. Perhaps I'll sleep a little.'

'I think I love you,' he whispered.

But in spite of that, she still managed to sleep. Just for a while.

* * *

Later in the evening they both woke up. At first they were happy just to lie there with their arms around each other.

'That was so good,' he said, 'but what now?'

'I don't know. We'll just have to see how things go.'

'Do you think we'll do this again?'

Now she had to consider. 'Well, in some ways it might not seem a good idea. There might be objections. But I like it so much, and you do too, so I suspect that whatever we decide we'll end up in bed again.'

'That's terrible,' he said with a grin.

'But some things have changed,' she went on. 'I now feel I have more rights here.' She felt the tensing of his body but decided to carry on anyway. 'So far you've largely kept me out of your kitchen. You've just cooked a wonderful meal and we left the dishes. So now I'm going to clear up.'

'There's no need! I'm quite capable of—'

'So am I. And I need to feel useful. So you lie here until I've finished and...' It seemed a bit odd to ask. 'And may I come and get back in bed with you?'

'Seems a good idea,' he said.

So they were going to sleep together that night, that was marvellous. Finn tried to keep calm and pretend that all was well. But he knew that their relationship had now moved into totally different territory. Making love to Alanna had been gorgeous but he wondered how it would affect them.

He read in bed a little, then got out and showered and cleaned his teeth. Alanna came back in half an hour, brought them a drink and said, 'I'm going to shower. I've cleared away what I can, put the dishes in the machine and made Eleanor's sandwiches. I'll shower in my room.'

Finn didn't show it, it was ridiculous, but he felt the tiniest touch of irritation at this. Eleanor's sandwiches were his job. He took pride in them. Then he worried about what he possibly could be worrying about.

Alanna quickly came back, slipped off her dressing-gown and was naked underneath it.

She slid into bed beside him. A quick kiss—and then moments later she was asleep. She had told him that she could sleep anywhere, get to sleep in minutes. But then he remembered she had been like that before. She slept like a cat—but like a cat she slept lightly.

He breathed deeply, pretending to sleep himself, but sleep wouldn't come. What was he to do now? He was getting to know Alanna, she was certainly a new person. And so was he. Technically—no, entirely—they were still married. He thought he still loved her. He knew now that she would never again be parted from Eleanor. The obvious thing would be for them to take up married life again. But there were two objections. First, he had been certain that he'd been in love before. As certain as now. And look at how that had ended. The shadow of the past still hung over him.

And Alanna—had she really lost the urge to move on? Could she settle down to apparently boring village life? Once she had told him, 'If there's a horizon, Finn, I want to see what's on the other side of it.' Benthwaite was surrounded by horizons. This was no use! He had work the next day. He'd have to sleep.

In the middle of the night there was a wail coming from the baby alarm. He waited for the second wail, was about to get out of bed. But from his side a naked figure rolled out of bed, pulled on his robe that hung on the door, and moved quickly to Eleanor's nursery. The wailing stopped, he could hear the low sound of comforting noises. He had to smile to himself. In many ways they were a threesome already. He slept well after that.

In fact, Finn slept so well that next morning he woke up to find the bed empty beside him and the alarm clock turned off. Alanna had woken before him and gone downstairs. He could hear rattling sounds from the kitchen. He was sorry she had gone. He'd half thought that if they woken up early enough, they might… No matter.

Shortly after that she brought him a cup of tea up and a happy voice said, 'You're not getting this treatment every morning. But breakfast is ready when you are.'

'I'll get Eleanor up,' he said. 'Because of you we're in plenty of time.'

Finn thought there was a different atmosphere at the breakfast table. It felt both more intimate and more awkward—which was difficult. And it was Alanna who broached the subject, drawing him aside so Eleanor couldn't hear them.

'Look,' she said, in a low voice. 'We both know that last night changed things between us. But I still think it best if we stick to the original agreement. I'm staying with you for three months— well, just over two months now—and then we review the situation. We've both been burned before, we don't want to rush into anything. We certainly don't want to tell anyone anything.'

'Agreed. No holding hands outside, no over-enthusiastic kissing, it's just that you are staying with me for a while.'

'Of course.' Eleanor started clamouring for attention so the conversation had to end. 'But what we do in the privacy of our—that is, of your—house, that's different.'

'I should hope so.'

* * *

As they drove to the cottage hospital together Alanna decided that she was glad that they'd had that morning's conversation. It hadn't sorted anything out, it had just put back the time for decision-making. And, she supposed, it would make that decision-making even more difficult. She wasn't yet in the mood for coping with difficulties.

But she couldn't call the previous night a mistake. It had been wonderful, it had brought back old happy memories and created new ones. But it had complicated the issue. She was still not sure what she wanted, how to organise her life now. It must centre on Eleanor. But Eleanor was now becoming more and more of her life, it was a given. Which meant she now had to think of Finn. And her relationship with him.

Last night he had said that he loved her. No, he had said that he thought that he loved her. All right, it had been a statement made after passion, but she thought he'd been sincere. The usual response after someone told you that they loved you was to reciprocate. But she hadn't. Not, she thought, because she didn't love him. She thought that she probably did. But to say that she loved him would mean a declaration that she was not sure she was ready to make. It would tie her future down.

She shrugged. They would carry on for a few more weeks, see how things went. At the moment she was enjoying her new life. And she felt that Finn was enjoying life more, too. He ought to be after last night!

Most mornings Finn did a round of the beds in the little hospital and Alanna had been given the job of accompanying him. There were eighteen beds in four wards. Some of the patients were older people who were having difficulty looking after themselves for a while. Some had had minor surgery and needed to recuperate. A few had been sent from the hospital in Carlisle to free beds there for more urgent cases.

'We've got a new patient now,' Finn said, flat-voiced. 'Enid Black. She was admitted last night through our A and E department. They decided there was no need to send her to Carlisle.'

He looked up from the notes he was studying. 'It says here that she fell downstairs, has bruises, contusions, a badly sprained ankle and a nasty gash to the skull. There were no immediate signs of concussion but she was kept in for observation anyway in case her condition deteriorated.'

He looked at Alanna, keeping his voice calm, and went on, 'She's been admitted two or three times over the past couple of years, once with a badly bruised face. She said she walked into a door.'

Alanna got the message. 'Don't tell me. A domestic.'

He shrugged. 'Probably, but there's no way I can prove it. I know her husband Joe, he's a brute. I tried to talk to her about it but she won't say anything. So there's nothing I can do.'

'It makes you angry, doesn't it?' Alanna said. 'You used to be able to distance yourself from this kind of thing. But you can't now.'

'I see Enid walking around town, we smile or stop and chat a bit. I feel responsible.'

'It's every doctor's problem,' Alanna said, 'and

I know it's hard. But you're a doctor, not God. There are some things you just can't deal with.'

'True. I know that but sometimes I don't feel it.' He looked at Alanna, an odd expression on his face. 'You might remember her from school. Her name was Enid Sommers then. She married the son of the landlord of the Red Lion. He's landlord himself now.'

'I remember her! A happy girl who never stopped talking.'

'Well, she's not happy any more. Come on, let's take a look at her.'

Enid was in a tiny side ward, which had only one bed. Alanna looked at the face peering from the pillows, turned away and winced. All right, the face was badly bruised—but there was more than that. The two of them were about the same age—but Enid looked ten years older. There were lines on her face, her hair was uncared for. And she had a general air of defeat. Enid had suffered.

After a few friendly words the two of them examined Enid. Finn thought that she wasn't too bad and could be discharged later. 'But you've got to take things easy for a couple of days Enid! No way can you work. I'll give you a note to say so.'

'All right, doctor. I'll do that.'

All three of them in the room knew that she was lying.

Enid was in pain but there was something about her that hadn't changed. She just couldn't stop talking. After a while she fixed her eye on Alanna. 'I know you,' she squeaked. 'You were Alanna Lightfoot, you used to be at school with me. We went on the school bus together. In fact, you used to go out with...' She looked at an uneasy Finn. 'You two used to go out together! And then, and then...I've seen doctor with a little girl—are you two married?'

'You're getting too excited Enid,' Finn said quickly. 'Take it easy for the rest of the day and I'll drop in again and see if you're fit to be discharged.'

He picked up her hand, appeared to be looking at the scratches on the inside of her wrist. 'How come you fell down stairs anyway? You've had more than a couple of bad accidents. Anything you want to talk about—in confidence, of course?'

Enid's expression changed. Alanna thought it half stubbornness, half fear. 'I just must be clumsy,' she muttered. 'It happens.'

'It does if you let it,' Finn said, 'and you know you don't have to. Like I said, I'll drop in later.' He and Alanna walked out of the ward.

'Not too many people have asked about you and me,' Finn said as they paced down the corridor, 'but you know that can't last.'

'I've seen quite a few people I recognise but I've tried to keep out of their way. It seemed the easiest thing to do. But now…'

'Now we might as well have told the town crier,' Finn said heavily. 'Something new for Enid to gossip about. It'll be all over the Red Lion bar tonight. Well, I suppose it's therapy for Enid.'

'A doctor to the end,' said Alanna, but she wasn't happy with the situation.

They worked together for the next couple of hours and then it was midmorning coffee time. He asked her if she'd make a fresh pot while he finished five minutes' paperwork.

She went to the staff lounge to make the coffee, poured herself a cup and sat there, thinking. There were two things. First, she—they—had never worked out what story they were going to tell people. So far they had managed to avoid lots of people who remembered her, but she realised that couldn't last. People would want to know where she had been for the last four years, how come Finn was looking after the baby alone, was the child hers, what was going to happen now? She didn't like the idea of being the subject of gossip.

The other upsetting thing was that now she remembered both Enid and Joe. They had both been happy, giggling schoolkids—though Joe had not been the brightest of lads. And now what had happened to them? She winced as she realised that their story wasn't too different from hers and Finn's. They had seemed to have had everything going for them—and look what had happened.

Of course, there had never been any physical violence between her and Finn. But she knew that verbal, mental violence could be just as lacerating. And both partners could practise it. She had been as guilty as Finn.

Finn entered the room just as she thought

this. 'You seem preoccupied,' he said. 'Anything wrong?'

Perhaps it was not a wise thing to do, but she told him. 'I remember Joe Black and Enid Sommers as a happy couple of kids. And look what they've turned into. Are you and I any different?'

There was silence for a moment and then he said, 'We can learn from our mistakes, Alanna, and I'm trying to. I can see some prospect of happiness ahead.'

He poured himself a coffee, stirred it slowly as he always did, then went on, 'You know I was worried when you turned up. I didn't know what was going to happen, how we'd get on. But now I'm certain that I'm happy that you're back.'

She nodded. 'That means a lot to me. And, Finn—things are working out better than I could have dreamed.'

'You mean Eleanor?'

'And you,' she said.

CHAPTER NINE

BECAUSE they had worked Sunday they both had Wednesday off. Finn was setting off early to go to a meeting in Carlisle with Harry as there were suggestions that the cottage hospital was going to be closed. The suggestions had to be fought and it looked like being a very long meeting.

Alanna was to be left to look after Eleanor. To get her up, feed her, take her to the crèche. Pick her up at night, make her tea, put her to bed. It was the first time that the two had been left together without Finn and she and Finn were… not worried but curious.

They told Eleanor on Tuesday night that she'd spend the next day with Alanna. Eleanor was happy. 'Lovely, lovely lovely!' she chanted. 'When I get home can we go riding at Jane's, Auntie Alanna? You like horses.'

This was something neither of them had expected and they looked at each other in consternation. 'I don't know if it's possible,' Finn said. 'Jane might be busy and…'

'I want to go riding with Auntie Alanna! You're going away and…' Just a small tear. Like all children, Eleanor was turning into an excellent manipulator.

Alanna and Finn looked at each other. 'Let me phone her,' Alanna said after a while. 'She did say that she'd be pleased to see us at any time. And she might find it easier to turn me down.'

'All right,' Finn said after a moment's thought. 'It's just that…'

She knew what he was thinking. 'Finn! I want you to hang onto your old friends. And if Jane fancied you, well, it just shows that she's got good taste. And I liked her, we got on. I'll phone right now.'

Jane sounded happy to hear from Alanna. 'Of course you'll be welcome. Come straight over when you're ready,' she said. 'Have you got any riding kit?'

'No.'

'Well, wear trousers and I'll look for a helmet for you.'

'But I couldn't expect—'

'I saw the way you were looking at the horses. You were pining. Just half an hour's canter will make you feel much better.'

'Right,' said Alanna, feeling quite pleased.

Another fine day, just the thing for riding. Obviously Eleanor had to have her ride on Daisy first. She was as delighted as ever. 'She's got a good seat,' Jane said critically. 'I think in time she'll be a real rider. But she's getting tired now, we'd better get her off. Now it's your turn.'

In spite of Alanna's objections, she was given a hat, led to the stables and introduced to a chestnut called Copper. Copper was beautiful and Alanna was thrilled when she saw her. She had ridden all sorts of animals abroad—most of them mules, donkeys, the common means of transport. But on a couple of occasions, in Australia and South America, she'd had the chance to ride real horses and she had loved it.

Jane carried Eleanor as Alanna climbed onto

Copper and they all walked to the big field. 'We'll watch. You walk and trot her a couple of circuits,' Jane suggested. 'Then why not have a go at a couple of the fences?'

Alanna did as Jane suggested, loving the exhilaration of the jumps. It struck her that eventually she and Eleanor could ride together. It would be another bond and… That was for the future. She didn't ride for too long. After all, she was there as a guest. She finished her ride and they all went back to the stables, Alanna took off Copper's harness and rubbed her down.

Then they went into Jane's lounge for tea and orange juice.

'You really must come riding with me some time,' Jane said once they'd settled Eleanor down in front of her favourite cartoons. 'Every now and then I need someone about my age to hack out with. I just couldn't tempt Finn—he's not into horses—so I wonder where Eleanor gets it from. You, I expect.'

'Me? But I'm just—'

Jane laughed. 'You're Eleanor's mother,' she said quietly. 'You only have to look at the two of you together to see that.' She poured them both a cup of tea. 'I suppose it's cards-on-the-table time. Obviously there's some story attached, you can tell me some time if you wish. I thought Finn was unattached. I suppose it's obvious that I fancied him. But he let me down very gently—in fact, only the day before you arrived. And when I saw him with you, the way he was looking at you, I knew why.'

Alanna found herself liking Jane's honesty. 'It's a long, awkward story,' she said. 'I'd tell you but I don't think it's over yet.'

'But you love him?' Jane asked.

'I think that's obvious. I love him all right. Well, I think I love him. But we have a...history.'

'History's the past,' Jane said. 'You have to live in the present. I had a husband and I loved him. He left me—not even for someone younger or prettier than me, but definitely richer. It was hard. But I got on with my life. I've met women who have been left by their husbands and have spent the rest of their lives being professional abandoned wives. Not me. I'm enjoying what I do and some day I'll meet another man.'

'That's the right attitude,' said Alanna. 'Look, there are people coming up the drive, presumably wanting to ride. We'd better go. Jane, this is difficult but can I pay you...'

'No, no, no! Just come again. Apart from anything else, last Easter Finn was so good with my daughter...I can never repay him. Just come again.'

As Alanna drove home with Eleanor she thought about what Jane had said. It was wrong to spend all your life feeling sorry for yourself. Take a risk if necessary. Then she thought about Enid and the consequences of her making a mistake. Two opposing arguments.

What should she do about Finn? Now she felt more confident about the future.

It was still early evening and the day had gone well so far. She drove home to find the customary pile of letters on the doormat. One specially thick one would be for Finn—doctors were always getting lots of thick letters. She put the mail in a neat pile on the corner of the kitchen table.

Then she went outside to spend an hour or so in the garden with her daughter. Every day she found herself loving her more and more. The shock of discovering she was a mother had now largely disappeared. But it had been replaced by an odd irrational fear. The thought of losing her daughter now she had found her seemed more than she could bear. But she knew it was a foolish fear and she was able to put it from her mind.

She thought about Finn as she sat on a blanket on the lawn, watching Eleanor playing with her dolls. He had said he loved her—he thought. Did she love him—well, of course she did. But…the memory of those evil days hung over her like a black cloud.

She thought he probably felt the same as she did about those days. But he was stronger than her. He had always been the one who could bend his head and wait for the storm to pass. Perhaps that was a good thing. Perhaps she could learn from him.

She had decided to have a meal ready for Finn when he came in. She knew he was a better cook than her—well, he'd had the practice. In the past few years many of her meals had been put together with only the poorest of ingredients. She felt her stomach. Was she getting fat as the result of his cooking? She thought not, she was working too hard.

She called Eleanor to come into the kitchen, gave her a banana and a drink and sent her to play where she could be seen. Then she looked in the fridge and the freezer. They'd have salad then chilli con carne and fruit afterwards. Chilli con carne was one of the meals that she knew she could cook well. Finn had liked it when she had cooked it before.

So she started to cook. And as she did so her eye fell on the pile of letters—the big one on the top—and she saw it was addressed to her. She blinked. Who knew that she was living here?

She opened the letter and out of it spilled other letters, cards, photographs. And there was a note, in Gabriel's large, distinctive handwriting. *I've been saving these for you. Just got back, learned your new address. I'll be in touch. Gabriel.*

This dismayed her a little. She didn't want to think of Gabriel right now. Her life had taken a different turning, she was having enough trouble with that. Still…. She looked through the letters, postcards and notes from old friends and acquaintances throughout the world. The headquarters of SAMS was her only permanent address, and she used it as a kind of post office.

It gave her an odd shock to realise how quickly she had forgotten her old life. She leafed through the mail he had sent her. There was a photograph of a camp she had worked in high in the Andes. Details of a drought in Australia. Letters from people she had treated who had gone on to live full lives.

She showed some of the postcards to Eleanor, who had wandered in and was mildly interested. Eleanor was most interested in a postcard of a cassowary from Australia. 'It's a big bird,' Alanna told her, 'bigger than Auntie Alanna.'

Eleanor was fascinated by that. 'Big bird,' she shouted. 'Big bird.' Alanna gave her the card.

Someone rang the doorbell. Alanna was curious, they didn't get too many casual visitors. Still, probably someone wanting Finn. She opened the door and looked at the visitor's smiling face in horror. What was Gabriel Buchanan doing there?

Well, she was living there, she supposed she was entitled to friends. She invited him into the kitchen, made a drink of tea for the two of them and they sat at the kitchen table. Eleanor came in and Gabriel made an instant friend of her. That was his way, he made a friend of everyone. But Alanna was suspicious.

'So what brings you here, Gabriel?' she asked. 'You're a long way from home.'

He shrugged. 'I had business over in Keswick, some kit we're ordering for abroad. I had to chase them up. And since I was in the area, I thought I'd drop in on an old friend. A spur-of-the-moment idea. You seem very comfortable here.'

'I am.'

She was still suspicious. Spur-of-the-moment stuff was not Gabriel's style. He planned everything. But he seemed quite amiable. He told her about his new plans for a centre high up the Amazon, and Alanna felt quite moved by his enthusiasm. She could see that he was a visionary but, unfortunately, like many visionaries, he was blinkered. Still, she listened. And she noticed how careful he was to speak to Eleanor every time she wandered into the kitchen.

There was a rattle at the front door. Eleanor shouted, 'Daddy,' and rushed off. Finn was back, earlier than he had said he would be. This was the last thing that Alanna had wanted. Then she felt angry at herself. She was entitled to her friends. And Gabriel had helped her in the past. Why shouldn't he call in?

Finn came into the kitchen carrying Eleanor and Alanna saw that he was surprised that she had a guest. She went over to kiss him, something she didn't ordinarily do. She saw his surprise, quickly masked, and realised it had not been the right thing to do. He must have wondered why she had kissed him. He might have wondered if she was feeling guilty.

'Finn, this is Gabriel Buchanan, an old friend of mine who I worked for in South America. He runs SAMS and he just dropped in to say hello.'

'And now I must say goodbye,' said Gabriel. 'You must have lots to do and I—'

'Where are you going?' asked Finn. 'Driving back to Leeds? You must have a meal with us first. Alanna, if you want to talk to your friend I'll cook and—'

'There's a meal already cooking,' Alanna said coldly. 'Plenty for all of us. If you go and get changed, we'll have a cup of tea here first and then I can chat in the living room to Gabriel for a while. We've got a few—'

'Couldn't we all chat in the kitchen?' asked Gabriel. 'I find it the centre of every home, and this is certainly a home.'

So they chatted in the kitchen. Mostly it was Finn and Gabriel talking, with Alanna chipping in occasionally. Finn saw the pile of cards and letters on the table and looked up at Alanna enquiringly. 'Look through them,' she urged. 'They'll show you the life I used to lead.'

He skimmed through them. 'Seems a very exciting life,' he said. He sounded interested but polite and she wondered if there was a slight edge to his voice.

This was something that she used not to like about him. When they had started their spiral downwards, he had developed the ability to say something apparently pleasant and yet leave a hint that he felt something different. She was just being paranoid!

Eventually she served the meal. She thought it was fine, both men praised it, but she didn't taste anything.

'I didn't realise that Alanna was part of a family group,' Gabriel said casually. 'I never would have offered her a job otherwise.'

'Job?' Finn asked quietly.

'In three, four months' time. We're opening a big medical centre in Peru, much more advanced than anything we've done so far. Much more civilised accommodation. We even have our own school. I wanted Alanna to be matron. She has the people skills necessary. But now I see—'

'Alanna has always been a free spirit. I suspect she will continue to be so,' said Finn with an apparent smile.

'Of course, of course,' said Gabriel. 'Dr Cavendish, I don't suppose I could interest you in a tour there? You're just the kind of doctor we want. There won't be much money but it's a satisfying life. And as I said, good accommodation, even a good school for little Eleanor here.'

'Tempting, but I think I'm settled here,' said Finn.

'Ah, a pity. Well, that was a very nice meal but I must be going.' He kissed Eleanor on the top of the head and said, 'A lovely child. You must be very proud of her.' Then he shook Finn's hand, a kiss on the cheek for Alanna and he was gone.

There was silence after he'd left. 'Now, that was an interesting meal,' said Finn.

An hour later she had put Eleanor to bed, after sticking the card of the cassowary to the wall above her bed. Eleanor had had a full day and was soon asleep. Then Alanna went downstairs to sit in the living room with Finn. This was a time she usually looked forward to. They might watch TV, listen to the radio, perhaps just read. But they were together and they were happy. But tonight something was wrong.

Finn was perfectly polite, but she sensed that there were feelings that he was keeping quiet and she hated it. So after a while she decided to do something about it.

She moved closer to him, took his hand, kissed him on the cheek. 'When we were arguing,' she said, 'you know, before, there were too many long silences, too little talking. Now I hope we can talk to each other. Be honest with each other, even if it hurts. I know you weren't very happy that Gabriel called. For that matter, neither was I. And I want to tell you first of all that it wasn't an accident. Gabriel is ruthless, a brilliant manipulator. He believes that what he is doing is right. So any way of getting his own way is fine.'

Finn was surprised. 'I could see he was an enthusiast, I liked him for that. But a manipulator?'

Alanna pointed at the pile of mail she had brought into the living room. 'He sent those. It was no accident that he arrived on the same day they did. He wanted me to look at them before he came. Perhaps get a bit dissatisfied.'

'It seems very devious for a man who is supposed to be running a charity.' Finn's voice was flat.

'I've got to be fair,' Alanna said. 'Some of the politicians he deals with, you have to be devious. But he shouldn't do it to people like us.'

Finn turned towards her, seized her two hands in his and stared into her eyes. 'We've been feeling our way forward,' he said, 'we're both cautious. Now, that is fine. But, as you said, we need to be honest with each other. I was a bit upset when he talked about you being a matron in Peru. He said he could see that your conditions had changed—but he also obviously expected you to take the job.'

'He told me about it before I met you again,' she muttered. 'I was thinking about it, I was very tempted, really expected to take it. But that was before I found out about Eleanor. She changes everything And it was also before… before I met you again.'

He nodded. 'Fair enough. Though I wish you had told me about the job.' Then he frowned. 'No, that's unfair. You did mention it but I'd forgotten. And you've had plenty of other things to think about recently.'

'And how,' she said with a small smile.

'Gabriel made it clear that you could still go to the medical centre, and that there would be a place for Eleanor there,' Finn went on. 'There would even be a place for me. Now, try to be honest, Alanna—and I know it's hard. Have you ever wondered about accepting the offer? Taking Eleanor with you?'

She could tell that this was the crucial question, his eyes were intent on her.

'I have wondered what we are going to do when our three months are up,' she said eventually. 'We both agreed we'd leave decisions until then. And I've thought of all possibilities, including going to Peru with Eleanor. But I'd never, never do anything to try to part the two of you. I can see what you mean to each other.' She took a deep breath. 'And there's something else. Not when I first got here, but now... I'm not sure that I want to be parted from you either.'

He laughed, wrapped his arms around her and kissed her. 'Not sure that you want to be parted from me? Alanna, I think that's the least passionate declaration of love that I have ever heard.'

'It's the best I can do,' she said indignantly.

'And it's absolutely honest. We've got quite a while to go yet. But things will improve.'

'I'm sure they will.' He glanced at the clock. 'Mrs Cavendish, it isn't too late and I'm not too tired. But I think I'll go to bed.' He looked thoughtful. 'I'm not sure I want anyone to come with me.'

'You're a beast,' she said, smacking him. 'You shouldn't make fun of me. Well, I'm sure I do want to go to bed with you. And when we get there I want to—'

He stopped her speaking by kissing her. 'Why not let's go together and you can show me what you want?' he said.

Next evening she showed him a letter. 'I've written to Gabriel,' she said. 'I've told him that there's definitely no chance of me accepting his job.'

He shook his head. 'I don't want you to send it,' he said. 'I think you should wait a while. We agreed to give each other three months. I want you to be able to make whatever decision you want then. Not burn your boats.'

'But I'm certain that—'

'No Alanna, do it for me. So I can be quite

certain that you made a free choice.' He grinned. 'And this is my small revenge on Gabriel for trying to manipulate us.'

'All right, then,' she said.

They didn't talk much about their future after that. Both were perfectly content to carry on in the way that they were. It wasn't a matter of re-establishing what they'd had before. Rather, they were getting to know each other, exploring what was new. They were different people from who they had been before. And they were falling in love again. Every day they seemed closer.

After a month she asked him if he'd like her to wear her wedding ring. Be Mrs Cavendish again instead of Miss Ward. He shook his head. 'I've thought about this,' he said. 'I've even spoken to the vicar about it. I'd like another wedding ceremony—the last one was all right but it was a bit rushed. I'd like to be married in church. The vicar says we could have a service of celebration, it would be the complete marriage service but we wouldn't sign the book. And we could have Eleanor as a bridesmaid.'

'She'd like that,' said Alanna. 'She'd think it was all laid on specially for her.'

'But remember, we agreed three months. I might want to ask you to renew our vows at the end of that time—or I might not.'

'Well, then,' she sniffed. 'I feel the same. If I'm asked I might say yes or I might say no. Or I might even make you wait for an answer. All is fair in love.'

'Now, isn't that true?' he said.

And she was enjoying the nursing. It wasn't efficiently impersonal as it had been in Leeds—where, of course, she knew it had to be. Here there was always time to chat to patients. Some of their beds were always occupied by older patients who could not look after themselves after an accident—usually a fall. Alanna especially enjoyed talking to them. And a couple of them remembered her as a girl.

'I remember you were always off on your bike with that young Finn,' one of them said slightly disapprovingly. 'And you in those shorts.' She tutted.

On a couple of occasions Alanna was called out on mountain rescue operations with Finn. Mike Thornton always asked for her specifically. He knew she was more than competent.

There was nothing really serious about either callout. This was usually the way, but the principle was always to go out and offer help. In the mountains something apparently trivial could quickly turn into something serious or even life-threatening.

So they had gone to help a school party come down off the fell. One girl had fallen three times already and hadn't been able to walk. She had been wearing grossly inadequate footwear. Mike had had a few crisp words with the school leader. They had stretchered down a game old lady who had fallen ten feet and torn ligaments in her leg. She had been very upset. 'I've been walking these hills for forty years now,' she'd told Alanna as she'd watched her leg being strapped up. 'I get angry at idiots who get into trouble through not knowing what they are doing or with poor equipment. But I do know what I'm doing.'

Alanna had looked at the old lady's boots, trousers and anorak. 'It's obvious that you know what you're doing,' she said. 'And we hope to see you doing more of it in a couple of months when this is healed. You're well kitted out. Falls can happen to anyone.'

'Hmm! But it's still annoying.' Faded but intelligent grey eyes had looked at Alanna. 'That doctor who examined me—he can't keep his eyes off you. Once men used to look at me like that. Is he your young man?'

'I think we've got something going.' Alanna had smiled at her. 'But neither of us quite knows what it is.'

Then one night there was a phone call at two o'clock in the morning. It had been an evil day, with high winds and cutting rain, and it was an even more evil night. Alanna heard the rattle of rain on the window, heard the wail of the wind outside. And she was so warm and comfortable in bed.

Finn took the call. She heard him muttering down the phone, felt the tension in his body as he came suddenly awake. He rolled out of bed, bent over to kiss her quickly. 'Mountain rescue callout,' he said. 'Sounds like a bad one. I would have liked you to come along but it's a bad night and you'd better—'

'I'm coming with you,' she said, throwing back the bed covers. Then she stopped to think. 'What about Eleanor?'

'It's sorted. Harry and I worked out a plan for this, we have a rota of emergency babysitters. In fact it's his turn. I'll phone him now.'

As ever, everything was very efficient. Harry and his wife turned up within minutes, track-suits over their pyjamas. They would sleep in Alanna's room—now largely unused. Eleanor knew them as Grandma Alice and Grandad Harry. She'd be quite happy.

Shortly afterwards the mountain rescue team arrived. They set off, the Land Rover shaking in the buffeting wind. As they drove to the dropping point Mike briefed them.

'This is a bad one. It's got to be us, weather conditions are too bad for the helicopter. A lad just managed to limp down the fellside, had to crawl some of the way. He got to the Glenister farm about three-quarters of an hour ago, knocked him up. Apparently there were two lads, they didn't tell anyone where they were going so they weren't missed.'

'Usual half-baked idiots,' someone in the back said.

'Anyway, they both fell. They were walking on Marshal's rake—not a good idea in this weather.'

Alanna knew it. It was a steep rocky rib that ran up the side of a hill called Bowderdyke. It was a fast way up the hill and there were great views of the estuary. But in bad weather it was dangerous.

'It was a bad fall, about fifteen feet or so. One is apparently badly bruised and dazed but he could move and he got down the mountain. The other, Terry Dent, has assorted small injuries, possible concussion and a complex fracture of the leg.'

Alanna winced. There could be bleeding into the tissues. And there was the danger of exposure so the sooner they got there the better.

'What about the lad who got to the farm?' Finn asked. 'Does he need attention?'

'Jack Glenister reckons not. Jack was in the army for nine years, he's seen plenty of injuries in his time. They've cleaned the lad up, fed him and put him to bed. Jack will deliver him to the hospital tomorrow.'

'Good. Do we know exactly where the injured lad is? Otherwise he might take some finding.'

'Fortunately we know. He's near a little cave halfway up the rake on the east side.'

'I know the cave,' Finn said. 'I've eaten my sandwiches there.'

They parked in Glenister's top field, after a bumpy ride up the track. When she got out Alanna reeled as the full force of the wind hit her. Finn caught her, his arm around her waist. 'Are you going to be all right?'

'I'm going to be fine. Finn, I've been in far worse weather than this.'

He looked at her, a slighter figure than the large men around her. She swayed again as a gust blew across the fields. Putting his head close to hers, he shouted, 'I'm still not sure that—'

'Forget it! The minute I can't cope you can send me back. But until then you need me and I'm coming.'

'I hope you aren't going to be as awkward

when we're married,' he muttered, and pushed his head inside her hood to kiss her quickly.

'I haven't said yes yet,' she pointed out. 'In fact, I haven't been asked properly.'

But there was work to do. They adjusted their lights, checked that they had all the equipment needed. 'We're not going up the rake itself,' Mike said, 'it's too dangerous. 'We'll skirt up the side of it. Keep close together, it'll be too easy to get lost in this.' And they set off. Mike led, Finn brought up the rear, the second most important man.

It was hard work, trudging up the path. There was no shelter, every gust pushed them to one side, made them stagger. Rain whipped across the little bits of their faces that were exposed, stinging though not really cold. Alanna hunched her shoulders, walked on. She had to show them that she was as good as them. Well, nearly as good.

They walked for about an hour, Mike setting a hard but not a stupid pace. And eventually the larger torch he was holding flickered across a body, lying near the mouth of a cave. It was a good thing they knew exactly where it was, it would have been easy to overlook in the dark. It wasn't a real cave, just an opening in a jumble of rocks. Thankfully the rocks provided Terry with some shelter from the elements.

While Mike and the rest of the team assembled the stretcher, Finn and Alanna huddled on each side of the still body. 'I'm Dr Cavendish, Finn Cavendish,' Finn said loudly. 'This is a nurse, Alanna Ward. We're going to get you down the mountain. How do you feel, Terry?'

The only answer was a moan. Terry was barely conscious. 'This is not looking good,' Finn muttered.

Terry's partner hadn't done a bad emergency job for someone who must have been quite badly shaken up himself. Terry was wrapped up tightly in two space blankets. There was an extra anorak over that. There was a scarf wrapped around his neck and head, a bobble cap on top on that. 'Going to take some undressing,' Alanna said.

But first there was the usual quick examination. 'Vital signs are low, pulse very erratic, breathing shallow, BP dropping,' Finn said, 'and he's lost an awful lot of blood. 'We'll start getting some plasma into him before I look at the leg.'

Alanna groped in the medical rucksack, handed him a hard collar before taking out the portable giving set. Together they fixed on the collar and in doing so they managed, just for a moment, to wake Terry up. 'It hurts,' he groaned.

'Terry, stay with us a minute! Can you move your toes? Can you feel them?'

There was a long pause and then the whispered words, 'I can wriggle them.'

'Good.' It wasn't certain, but it suggested that there were no spinal injuries—not yet anyway. They'd still have to take great care in moving him.

Now the broken leg. Alanna pulled away the space blanket, looked at what was below. Terry's partner had done the best he could, tying the two legs together so the injured one was in effect splinted. But the injured leg was still shorter than the whole one. He had put a rough dressing over where the bone had protruded through the flesh—a scarf, Alanna thought. She reached into the rucksack for an emergency dressing. This was just a holding process, keeping things from getting worse. Terry needed a hospital theatre.

Meanwhile Finn had ensured the injured leg was immobilised. 'Best we can do for the moment,' he said. 'Let's get him out of here.'

It was hard getting Terry onto the stretcher without causing too much pain or risking more damage. In the end as many as possible gathered round the still body and they passed him from hand to hand till he was outside the cave. Then he was placed in the stretcher.

'The sooner we get him to hospital the better,' Finn said. 'He needs a surgeon, urgently. We make best speed—but we don't hurry.'

'So let's move,' said Mike.

CHAPTER TEN

IT WAS hard work carrying him downhill. There was the occasional inevitable trip when the patient was jerked and he groaned. It wasn't a bad thing. When a patient was completely silent, it could mean he was slipping into unconsciousness. A couple of times Finn called a halt, quickly checked his patient. Not that there would be much more that he could do. So they pushed onwards through the wind and rain until the ground flattened out and they knew they were only ten minutes' walk from the Land Rover.

It had happened so many times. It was a danger they were well aware of—most accidents happened in the last few minutes of a journey. Walkers grew confident, relaxed when they thought they were near the end.

Not this group. They were both cautious and

well trained. But it was typical that it happened on the last stretch. Alanna saw it happen. They were walking through an old gateway, Finn one of the front stretcherbearers. He must have stood on a loose stone, the stone gave way. Finn lurched into the stone gatepost and stumbled onto his knees. But he didn't let go of the stretcher, try to save himself.

Alanna heard his sudden intake of breath, heard his sudden gasped request to the others. 'Hold it a minute.' She moved to his side, shone her headlamp onto his leg—and winced. As he had skidded sideways he had caught his leg on a protruding spike of sharp metal—already there was blood showing through his trousers.

'It's not too bad,' Finn said. 'We've got to get this man to hospital.'

It wasn't her place but Alanna intervened. 'That leg needs an emergency dressing,' she said. 'It needs it now. Why don't you four carry on to the vehicle? I'll get a bandage on this and we'll catch you up.'

'It's not far now,' Finn said, 'and in the Land Rover I can—'

Alanna is right,' Mike cut in as he looked at the now bloodstained leg 'We'll do as she suggests. It'll take us a while to settle this lad in the vehicle. You two will be there before we're ready to move off.' Mike was the team leader. They had to do as he said. He took Finn's place at the stretcher and they moved off.

Alanna was left in the middle of the night in pouring rain and howling wind, and the man she loved was in pain. So what? She was an emergency nurse.

She took the wet bandana from around her neck and told him to hold it against the wound—it would slow down the bleeding. Then she eased the rucksack from his back and rummaged through the medical supplies until she found the antiseptic powder and an emergency dressing. 'Undo your trousers and push them down, ' she said.

He did as she said. 'I hope no one sees me like this,' he said, managing to joke. 'Trousers around my knees in the middle of a field in a storm.'

'When I've finished we'll take photographs. Sell them for charity. Now, this might hurt a bit.'

She tried to keep her voice normal as she looked at the gash in his thigh. It wasn't too dangerous but it would be painful. There was no time for fancy measures. She covered the area with antiseptic and then slapped on an emergency dressing and bound it tight. 'Right, pull your trousers up, that's all we can do here. But I want a closer look when we get home.'

'Yes, nurse. Now, can we go, please?' How could he still joke? The leg must be causing him agony.

She glanced at her watch. The treatment had taken exactly five minutes—time well spent. 'Now we go,' she said, 'and you don't hurry.' So they set off, he still trying to hurry and she determined that he would not do more than he should.

In fact, their timing was perfect. The team had just eased their patient into the Land Rover when they arrived. Finn insisted on another quick look before the vehicle drove off, and as soon as they were moving he phoned for an ambulance and asked for it to be waiting at the cottage hospital. One of the other members of the team was a little upset at this.

'Are you sure we need to send him to Carlisle, Finn? Can't you see to him? We've got the lad off the mountain, it would be great if we could finish the job.'

Finn shook his head. 'I know my abilities,' he said. 'That leg is a bit more than I can cope with. It needs a full theatre and a consultant orthopaedic surgeon. Be happy we've got him down.'

'Right, then.'

It was, of course, the right decision. But Alanna could remember the time when Finn would have been far more irritated at having to hand over a case. He had changed—and she liked him for it.

The ambulance had just arrived at Rosewood as they pulled into the forecourt. The patient was swiftly transferred. Finn carefully wrote out his observations so far and handed them to one of the paramedics. The ambulance drove off—and the rescue team stood there feeling a vague sense of anticlimax.

Alanna glanced at the sky. There was the beginning of a bleak dawn. The Rosewood night sister came out and said, 'I've organised some tea. You need a hot drink before you all go home.'

'Sounds a great idea,' said Mike.

'I'm taking Finn to the A and E department,' Alana said. 'I want another look at his leg. But tea is be a good idea. And, Finn, you take yours with sugar. Two spoonfuls.'

He smiled. 'I'm not going into shock,' he told her.

'Now, where have I heard that before? Usually from some fellow two minutes before he collapses on the floor. Drink your sweet tea and like it.'

So he took his tea to the A and E department. She made him take a painkiller then gently took off the temporary dressing. The wound needed to be irrigated, inspected for dirt or rust and then coated with antiseptic. He leaned over to look. 'I don't think it needs suturing,' he said. 'Butterfly stitches should do.'

She had to remind him, 'The doctor who treats himself has a fool for a patient. But I agree. I'll hold it together with butterflies.' It gave her an odd kind of pleasure to tend to the man she loved.

They went back to the main hall. The rest of the team was still there, drinking more tea and talking quietly. No one really seemed to want to go home. They were a team, they had worked well together, it was a pity to part. But, still, they had jobs in the morning.

'A good job,' said Mike. 'We did well.'

There was a general rumble of agreement.

'I'll phone the hospital later on today and find out how the lad's doing,' said Finn. 'I'll let Mike know and he can tell you all.'

'I'll do that,' said Mike. 'But now let's go home.'

They tried to be quiet as they entered their house but Harry was awake anyway. He looked at the state of them both, wet and weary. 'Right, you both take the morning off. There'll be no trouble covering for you. Later on one of you can get Eleanor up and I'll take her into the crèche.'

'We're all right really, Harry—' Finn started, but Harry interrupted him.

'I'm senior partner of this practice, you do as I say. Now, go and get a couple of hours' sleep.'

That seemed like a great idea to Alanna. She led Finn to the bathroom, told him that he couldn't have a shower, he had to have a bath and hang his leg over the side so as not to wet his dressing. 'And as you're in a bit of a state, I'll help you wash.'

'That'll be nice,' he said.

They dumped their wet clothes in the hamper in the bathroom, and she helped him wash, as promised. Then, naked, they both went to peep at their sleeping daughter. It made what they had been doing all seem worthwhile.

It was so good to get back into bed. Finn wrapped his arms around her, kissed her cheek. 'Great team, aren't we?' he muttered.

'A great team. And we're good at medicine, too.'

She was happy as she went to sleep.

The hospital was always busier in summer. The population of the little town expanded to four or five times its normal number with tourists. This was the time when the townspeople made their money. And sometimes it seemed to Alanna that the visitors left their brains at home. People did things, took risks that they would never have done at home. The little A and E department was filled with cases that could have been prevented with a little care.

Most cases, of course, were minor, and the nursing staff was easily able to cope. But sometimes they needed a doctor and often they'd send for Finn. Alanna loved working with him. They were a team.

They had a week of glorious, intense sunshine. And although there had been no end of warnings about the dangers of too much exposure, of the benefits of sunblock, of the increase in dangerous UV rays because of global warning, no one appeared to be paying any attention. The department treated a constant procession of grizzling children and of uncomfortable adults with large areas of scarlet or already peeling skin.

'We ought to buy shares in the firm that makes calamine lotion,' grumbled one of the nurses. 'They must be making a fortune, the amount we're using.'

'True,' Alanna agreed. 'But think—they must be making a loss on selling sunblock. I don't think anyone's buying it.'

As ever, there were a couple of serious cases of sunburn, people with high temperatures and nausea. Alanna sent for Finn who ordered them both to be kept in overnight.

Then there was the multitude of sprains, scratches, stings. And the campers who seemed to make a habit of burning their fingers. But Alanna enjoyed the work. She was happy.

It was recognised that, as in so many of the A and E departments throughout the country, late Friday and Saturday nights were the worst. That was when the drunks came in— often accompanied by their equally drunken friends. Things could get unpleasant. But cunning Harry had arranged that the trouble would be minimal.

Simon Malton worked two twelve-hour shifts on Friday and Saturday nights in the A and E department. In his eight-year stay in the army he had been trained as a paramedic. Now he was studying medicine at Newcastle and the money he earned at Rosewood came in very handy.

Simon was six feet four inches tall—and was

also broad. No one argued while Simon was around. He didn't argue. He just stood and looked. And that was enough.

So Alanna was happy at work, was happy with Finn and with her daughter. Life was good. And before she realised it, she had been in Benthwaite for two months. It came as a shock.

She was finished breakfast with Finn one morning while Eleanor played within sight, and softly Finn said, 'Only four weeks to go, Alanna, and then your time is up.'

'Time? What time?'

'Don't you remember? We agreed that you'd stay here for three months to get to know Eleanor and then you'd decide what you wanted to do next.'

'Hmm,' she said quietly. 'I also remember a solemn decision to keep out of your bed. That decision seems to have evaporated.'

He waved his egg spoon in the air. 'Entirely your fault. Anyway, somehow or other, by accident or design, we seemed to have worked out some kind of joint life that suits us both. I want to carry on like this—only make it more permanent. And I hope you do, too. I'd like to celebrate our getting together.'

'What had you in mind?' Alanna hadn't been ready for this. She was feeling a little unsure.

'I want Eleanor to call you Mummy. I want you to start wearing your wedding ring. I want us to arrange a wedding celebration at church. I want us to be Mr and Mrs Cavendish properly.'

'Quite a programme.'

'That's only the first half of the programme. There is another thing.'

She saw his face, half serious, half joking. 'What other thing?'

He looked over at their daughter, who was engrossed in her dolls. 'Eleanor's lonely. She needs a brother or sister, perhaps even both. What do you think?'

It was the last thing Alanna had expected. 'Finn, you can't just suggest something like that to me over breakfast!' She was genuinely shocked. She sat there, thinking. Of course, it was an obvious idea. They'd never talked about it but if they were to stay together...

Eventually she said, 'I suppose for most

women of my age, that's a normal thing to think about. But for four years I put it out of my mind. I'd had a child and thought it had died. I wasn't going to go through that trauma again. So talking of a baby now is…well, a bit of a shock. I need to get used to the idea.'

She was sad when she saw the look of vague disappointment on his face. But he waved his spoon again and said, 'Remember, only a month left! Or it's bags packed and you're off.'

Work in A and E that morning was as hard, as enjoyable as ever, but she couldn't give it the same concentration as usual. She thought about what Finn had said. The last two months had been the most shocking but the most wonderful of her life. She loved Eleanor, couldn't imagine life without her. The initial frenzy of delight had now gone, replaced by something much deeper. And there was Finn. He had come second. After she had found out about Eleanor he had had to come second. But now he was central to her life. She had come to love him, a love she knew to be deeper than that she had felt before. But…but what?

That morning, when he had talked about having more children, he had scared her. She had put all thought of having more children out of her mind, the heartache was just too great. But then she'd discovered that she already had a child—there was no need for heartache. And there was no reason why she shouldn't have another—or even two or three!

When she had first found out about Eleanor she had agreed to Finn's plan for a three-month wait before they came to any decision. Now the time for decision-making was coming close—and she was frightened at the prospect. And to consider having more children—that was planning her entire life! She didn't know if she could decide. She was frightened.

That night she came home first as Finn had to stay at the practice to talk to some visiting health professional. Keeping an eye on Eleanor, who was playing happily in her Wendy house, Alanna fetched the packet that Gabriel had sent. She hadn't really looked at the contents. There were postcards, photographs, drawings, letters, mementoes from the time she had been away, travelling. Away from Finn.

She supposed she should put them in some sort of an album. As she looked through pictures of half-forgotten places and letters from friends now lost, happy memories came back. She smiled, remembering her careless, freewheeling days. Not that she would change her present life to get them back…

She heard the door open, Finn was back unexpectedly early. Almost guiltily she tried to sweep the letters and photographs back into the envelope. Of course, he caught her. Things were made worse by the fact he didn't seem to mind.

'Looking over old times?' he asked pleasantly. 'I suppose you must miss them sometimes.'

'I'm happier now,' she said. She meant it, it was true. But she hadn't said it with much conviction.

As she finished cramming the papers back into the envelope she realised that he had asked very little about her past life. And she hadn't volunteered very much. For absolutely no reason whatsoever, that made her feel more guilty than ever.

He sat down at the kitchen table opposite her. Obviously he had something to say to her that was important to him—she could tell by the tone of his voice, by the way his eyes searched her face.

'I know it's wrong to mix business with pleasure,' he said. 'Or, in this case, business with business. But this morning I had the vicar in, just for a check-up. When we were chatting I asked him about the wedding service again and he said that he'd love to do it. But it would be a good idea to book early. A lot of people apparently want to be married at St Mary's.'

'It must be nice to be popular,' she said. She didn't want it to be, but her voice seemed strained. And Finn noticed.

'Everything all right?' he asked, the concern in his voice obvious. 'You seem a little bothered.'

She shook her head. 'It's just that…this getting married, going back to the way we were, well, we've only really got together over the past two months, haven't we? I know we said three months and then we'd plan the future. But don't you think that's a bit too short?'

Now his voice altered, became harsher. 'No,' he

said. 'I think we know enough about each other to be certain now. I know I'm certain, Alanna. I love you, I think you love me. I want to get married in church, and then, not too long after, I want us to think about another child. Whatever we have together, I'm certain that another baby would make it even more wonderful.'

She wasn't sure why she said it, it just came out. 'Well, I'm not entirely sure. The last two months have been fantastic, but I think it's too short a time. Can't we extend it to six months? Stay as we are until then? We're happy now, aren't we?'

'We're happy now,' he agreed, 'but I think we could be happier.'

She knew he wasn't happy but couldn't think of anything to say. 'I'll put these away,' she said, taking her envelope, 'then I'll make Eleanor's tea.'

She felt lost.

Finn was called out late that evening to go to A and E. A farm worker had fallen off a barn roof and he had broken ribs. Finn sent for the radiographer, who took X-rays, then strapped up the man. For a while it took his mind off things.

He admitted the man, told his family that everything would be all right and then set off for home again. But for some reason he was restless.

He didn't want to go straight home to Eleanor and Alanna. And that was a first. Instead, he drove up the hill just out of town and parked where he could see across the valley, the lights of the little town sparkling below him. He climbed out of the car, sat on a convenient bench and wondered.

He'd thought everything had been going well with Alanna. He'd thought both of them had changed and were looking forward to a life together. That morning he had deliberately talked about babies, he had thought the idea would delight her. It delighted him. But he had been wrong and he had been disappointed at Alanna's apparent lack of enthusiasm.

Had she really changed? Was the old, wild, wandering Alanna coming back? He had thought not. Anyway, there was Eleanor to settle her, no one could doubt the love they felt for each other. She couldn't wander with Eleanor, could she? The thought gave him some small satisfaction—and then he winced. Maybe she *could* wander with Eleanor. If she became matron at this clinic that Gabriel had told her about, there would be a place for Eleanor, too. That thought was too evil to contemplate!

It would mean that he'd have to… No, it couldn't get that far. He'd fight and… Panic-stricken, he wondered if they would end up battling it out in court. He remembered the steely determination she could show. He'd seen little sign of it recently, but that was because there had been no need for it. He suspected it was still there.

Feeling confused, angry, lost, he got in the car and drove home.

'I phoned the hospital,' Alanna said as she poured him a cup of tea. 'They said that you left half an hour ago.'

He answered honestly, which was perhaps not a good thing. 'I went up to Drover's Point and thought about things.'

'Thought about what things?'

He shrugged. 'Just life in general.'

It was not a good answer. When they went to

bed that night she turned her back to him and apparently went straight to sleep.

Afterwards, Alanna decided that that had been the beginning of a downhill slide that neither of them appeared to be able to stop. She knew that the next thing was her fault—but after the tiniest of worries it was something that she felt she had to do. She wondered when would be the best time to ask him. And then wondered why she should bother. This was her right. Eleanor was her daughter.

So she asked him while they were getting Eleanor ready the next morning. 'Finn, is it recorded anywhere that I am Eleanor's mother?'

He frowned. 'Well, you're still married to me and I am now registered as her father. There was rather a lot of unpleasant legal wrangling as to what to do. Fortunately, no one wanted Eleanor. No one but me, that is. The woman who was thought to be her mother had no partner, had no real family. I know that Social Services often has a hard job to do. But at one stage it seemed as if they were taking a positive delight in being obstructive. But I got a lot of help from the hospital, which was anxious to avoid a scandal and which was worried about being sued. Which I had no intention of doing.'

'It must have been hard for you,' she said sincerely. 'I feel for you. But the result is that she is now your daughter, but not quite mine.'

He said nothing, just looked at her. After a moment he went to his desk, fetched a folder and placed it in front of her. 'All the documents are here,' he said, 'mostly prepared by the solicitor who acted for me. If you want to get in touch with him, I'll happily sign anything that acknowledges your claim to Eleanor. But, Alanna, I really don't see why it's necessary.'

She shook her head. 'I know that, Finn! I just would like…something I could look at. You can see that, can't you?'

'If you say so,' he said. But she knew he didn't mean it.

They were both working harder than ever. Alanna spent most of her time at the cottage hospital, Finn seemed to spend more time in the actual practice building. She saw him at least once every day at work—but often it was just for a moment. And she missed working with him. They still made love as ardently as ever. But something, she couldn't tell what, had come between them.

After a fortnight he asked her again if she had made up her mind about the future. Only two weeks before the three months was up.

Alanna had had a particularly hard day. One of the older patients had died, an old lady who remembered her as a little girl. Alanna had nursed her, had enjoyed chatting to her about old times—and now she was gone. They had not been very close, but Alanna still felt that the day had been hard.

She hadn't told Finn about it. So he may have been surprised when she snapped at him, 'I really can't think about it right now. I need more time. I'd like another three months, but you think that's too long. So let's compromise. If not three months then I'll meet you halfway. I need another six weeks, OK?'

'Whatever you need, Alanna. If you need the time—then of course you may have it. Six extra weeks—that's two months from now.' His voice was quiet and she hated herself for making him suffer. But for some reason she couldn't say so.

Nothing much happened for a while. Both were aware that they were drifting apart, neither could work out why. Then Gabriel phoned, said he'd be in the area again and asked if he could call, just for a cup of tea perhaps. Alanna said of course, but made sure that Finn would be in the house when Gabriel came.

Gabriel called—complete with an African doll for Eleanor—and was as charming as ever. He told Alanna not to worry about turning down the job he had offered her, but said there'd always be a place for her at SAMS. And one for Finn, too. Now, next week there was to be a reception in Leeds for SAMS, would they both like to come?

'It's kind of you Gabriel,' Finn said politely, 'but at the moment I just can't spare the time. But Alanna can come.'

'I've got work, too,' Alanna pointed out.

'Mustn't think of yourself as indispensable,' Finn said cheerfully. 'I'm sure we can arrange a substitute for a couple of days.'

So it was agreed. But when Gabriel had gone Alanna felt that she had to speak to Finn. 'I wish you hadn't said that I could go,' she said. 'I am capable of answering for myself.'

'Sorry. I was just trying to be helpful.'

So she went to the reception. She met a few old friends and enjoyed herself. And when she returned she told Finn how much she had enjoyed herself.

What was happening to them both? Neither seemed capable of stopping it. Alanna wondered if her old self was returning. Was she as awkward as before, ready to fight at the smallest slight? And was Finn reverting to his old self, polite but silent, refusing to get involved, to argue? Thank God they hadn't yet had one of their old terrible rows. That would be the end.

It nearly was the end. She came back from shopping one evening to find a calmly smiling Finn. 'You've just missed a telephone call from Gabriel,' he said. 'He said that he knew you probably wouldn't be interested but that SAMS was running a training course this coming weekend and one of the lecturers has just fallen ill. He wanted to know if there was any chance of you giving a couple of talks. Your input would be invaluable. I said I was sure that you'd come.'

It was one of the hardest things she had ever done, not to start a screaming match there and then. But she contented herself with saying, 'If you've told him that I'm coming, I'd better just phone and confirm it.' And she did.

She hired a little car to take her to Leeds and set off on Friday evening. She had prepared her material, she knew that what she had to say was valuable and would be of use. But she hated leaving Eleanor. And she hated leaving Finn. Why couldn't things be as they had been before? Just before she'd left, Finn had said with the calm smile that could irritate her so much, 'You told me that Gabriel was a devious man. What if you get drawn in this weekend and he offers you a job?'

'I'll just have to think about it, won't I? See if it's a really good offer.' A moment later she wished she hadn't said it. But Finn had turned and gone back into the house.

* * *

In fact, she enjoyed the course. Her lectures went well on Saturday morning and she was looking forward to enjoying the outdoor training sessions that would follow. It was like reliving old times. But already she knew that they *were* old times. Most people on the course were younger than her, had no ties. She was now a different woman, she had a child and a husband. She would sort things out with Finn as soon as she got back. If he still wanted to marry her, if he still wanted her to have his children—then she did, too. After all, she loved him.

In the afternoon they went on a navigation exercise on the Yorkshire moors. One of the requirements was that they didn't take mobile phones. They had to work together, rely on their own knowledge. It went well and she enjoyed it, but when their minibus drew up outside the course centre, there was an anxious Gabriel running towards them. He pulled her out of the minibus, thrust a phone towards her.

'Finn's been phoning you every fifteen minutes. It's urgent you phone back.'

She did so. At first Finn's voice sounded calm but she knew him and could detect the thread of terror underneath what he was saying. 'Eleanor's had an accident. We need you here at once. She's been asking for you.'

'Accident? What…? How…? Finn, is she all right?' She knew she was screaming, the others looking at her in dismay.

'Alanna! We can't afford to get hysterical. Just get here as quickly as you can.' His voice was cracking, she could feel the effort he was making to remain calm. And that made her feel worse.

'What happened to her? How is she?'

'Well, she's alive. A slate fell off one of the houses in the town. It hit her on the head and shoulder. She has a fractured skull and she lost a lot of blood. Alanna, this is serious.'

This couldn't happen! She had just rediscovered her daughter. She couldn't be…she couldn't be taken from her again. But somehow she found the strength to speak. 'Where are you?'

'The pediatric department at Carlisle. I've got

Ian Kershaw, the paediatric surgeon, standing by. He's going to operate as soon as he thinks Eleanor has stabilised. Alanna, Eleanor was asking for you.'

'Finn…Finn… I can't… What if she…?'

'Alanna!' Somehow his voice became firm again. 'This is the time to be a nurse, a professional. Don't get into that car unless you're certain you can drive safely. Eleanor needs you alive! And, God knows, so do I.'

She stood there, aware she was shaking and not knowing how to stop. Then she said, 'All right, I'm on my way. Be there as soon as I can…as soon as I can get there safely.' She rang off.

Gabriel had been listening. He said, 'You're not driving. I'm a better driver than you, I've got a faster car. I'm taking you. Don't worry about packing, don't worry about your car. We can deal with it.'

'But, Gabriel, the course—'

'People come before courses. I've always believed that. Now, there's my car, get in it.'

She was vaguely aware that Gabriel was indeed a good driver. She said nothing, just stared out of the car window, watched towns, villages, hills rush past. But it still seemed for ever before they were pulling up outside the hospital.

She had visited there before, she knew the way, and the moment the car stopped she was running across the forecourt, along corridors, into the paediatric reception area.

'Eleanor Cavendish! Where's Eleanor Cavendish? I'm her mother.'

The clerk at Reception had obviously been briefed. She frowned and said, 'I was told to expect a Miss Ward, who would—'

'Ward, Cavendish, what does it matter? I'm Eleanor's mother!'

The clerk picked up the phone and said, 'A lady saying she's Eleanor's mother is here.' She didn't ask Alanna to sit down—she knew it would be foolish.

Alanna heard a door open behind her. She turned and there was Finn.

She didn't know what she was feeling. A maelstrom of emotions whirled within her. First there was pity for the man she loved. In his face she could see the terror that she felt herself. He could lose his child—they could lose their child—and it would be more than either of them could bear. Then there was a vague feeling of comfort. She was with Finn now. Whatever pain there was, he would help her through it. He was a man she could lean on, a man who would comfort and support her. But what about Eleanor?

She rushed to him, felt his arms wrap around her, felt the roughness of his chin against her cheek, heard the deep breath he took. Things weren't better now—but at least she had someone to share her pain.

'Finn, how is she? Where is she?'

'She's in Theatre. Ian's working on her skull. He decided to do it at once rather than wait to see if things got worse or better. Alanna, this is…is serious.'

Her heart went out to him as she heard the quaver in his voice. But she still took strength from him being there.

'What does Ian say?'

'He's a surgeon, you know they won't say anything definite. He just says he'll do the best he can and that she's got a fighting chance.'

A fighting chance? Was that all? 'Finn, if she, if she…if she isn't with us, that's…'

'I was with her in the ambulance and she came to for a minute. She asked for Auntie Alanna. Then she was unconscious again.'

'And I wasn't there!'

Someone else entered the reception area, footsteps echoed behind them. She turned. It was a pale-faced Gabriel. 'Alanna, Finn, please, tell me Eleanor is all right?'

'She's in Theatre now,' said Finn. 'We'll know later.'

'I'll pray for her. Alanna, don't worry about what's left behind, I'll sort it out. Will you let me know…how things are? Perhaps tomorrow some time?'

'I'll phone you,' said Alanna. 'Finn, Gabriel drove me here. He thought I wouldn't in any state to.'

'That was kind of you, Gabriel,' said Finn. 'And we will phone you tomorrow.'

'I'll be thinking of you.' Gabriel kissed her on the cheek, shook Finn's hand and left.

'Now, I want to know exactly—' Alanna started, but was interrupted by an orderly.

'Dr Cavendish, Mr Kershaw says he's finished. Would you like a word with him?'

'How's Eleanor?' Alanna burst out.

The orderly smiled. He obviously liked bringing good news. 'She's being moved into Intensive Care. Mr Kershaw seemed quite... I'm sure he'll tell you.'

They were led down more corridors and eventually found Ian Kershaw sitting on a bench, still in blood-stained scrubs, His mask was around his neck. He looked tired.

'Finn, Alanna, I've done what I could. The damage has been repaired. She's not getting any worse. But you can't go messing with a four-year-old child's body and not expect any reaction. Now she's got to recover, and that's as much up to her as it is to medicine. If she makes it through to morning, she should be OK. But it's up to her.'

'Can we see her now?' Alanna asked.

The surgeon looked surprised. 'Of course you can,' he said. 'She's in Paediatric Intensive Care, they're expecting you. I'll be down there myself in an hour or so. You know the way?'

'I know it,' said Finn.

Alanna had been in many intensive care units, she knew the purpose of the battery of instruments behind the bed, knew why all the tubes were attached to her daughter. But it was her daughter and so it was frightening. And her baby looked dwarfed by it all. A tiny white face under a turban of bandages.

Suddenly a memory crashed back. Four years ago. It was the morning after she had given birth, she was still sore, her head still ached from the injury it had sustained. And she was shown the body of her dead baby—she thought. She could hold it back no longer. She put her head on Finn's shoulder and wept, the sobs seeming as if they were torn from her soul.

Finn put his arms around her, drew her to him. After a while she took some comfort from it.

In time the tears disappeared. Finn took out his handkerchief, dried her eyes. 'We have to wait,' he said. 'But she's a strong child.'

'She's a strong child,' Alanna repeated. 'And

you're a good father. You've fed her well, kept her fit. She's strong enough to win this fight.'

A nurse brought them two chairs and they sat side by side. For a while she did nothing but stare at her baby. But she was a nurse—as Finn was a doctor. They studied the dials recording Eleanor's vital signs. Eleanor was holding her own. Just.

They sat holding hands. They waited. The nurse brought them cups of tea, they thanked her and let the tea go cold. After an hour Ian Kershaw came in, studied the recordings and nodded. 'All quite reasonable so far,' he said. Quite reasonable? This was her daughter's life!

They continued to sit, holding hands. They continued to wait. Occasionally a nurse looked in, asked them if there was anything she could get them. But they wanted nothing. All they could do was wait.

Behind the bed the instruments measured Eleanor's battle for life. Occasionally the pointers wavered, which was quite normal. But then there seemed to be a gradual movement downwards. Eleanor's strength was failing.

The nurse came in, looked at Eleanor.

Alanna could tell that under that professional calm she was uneasy. The nurse said, 'Perhaps I ought to bleep Mr Kershaw. Nothing to worry about yet but…'

Softly, Finn said, 'I'm a doctor, my wife is a nurse. We can tell that there's something to worry about.'

The nurse nodded. 'I know. But why don't you both try to talk to your daughter? It might help.'

'But she's unconscious!'

'I've worked in Intensive Care for years. You'd be surprised what people manage to hear when they're thought to be unconscious. They've told me about it afterwards. Besides, it might help you.'

It couldn't do any harm. Alanna leaned forward. 'Eleanor, Eleanor, this is…' This was who? Suddenly Alanna didn't want to be Auntie Alanna any more. 'Eleanor, this is your mummy. Can you hear me? This is your mummy.'

Behind her she heard Finn's gasp of surprise. But she went on, 'You had a nasty bang on your head and Mummy and Daddy want you to try and get better. You can hear me, I know, so get better and then we'll…then we'll go to the beach again and we'll go riding again and we'll do all sorts of things. You and me and Daddy. Eleanor, this is your mummy.'

She didn't know what she said. She talked, said anything, just so long as Eleanor could— might—hear her voice. And every second sentence she told her daughter that her mummy was speaking. Finn spoke too, both of them willing their precious daughter to respond.

She was surprised when she felt a hand on her shoulder and looked up to see the nurse. 'Things are looking up,' the nurse said. 'I think it worked. Now, sit by your husband and I'll fetch you both another cup of tea. And this time you're to drink it.'

So they drank their tea and they watched their daughter and the dials above her and saw certain signs that Eleanor's condition was improving. At midnight Ian Kershaw came in, a broad smile on his face. 'Things are looking good,' he said. 'Though I'm sure you don't need me to tell you that. Now, there's no point in your staying here any longer. We've got bedrooms for parents who stay overnight, there's one waiting for you. Come on, this is doctor's orders, you're to go to bed. There's going to be quite a bit of work for you in the future. And if there's any change, the nurse will fetch you at once.'

So they went to the little hospital bedroom.

'I think Eleanor's going to be all right so we're not going to say anything, not going to talk,' Finn said. 'For tonight we just lie in each other's arms, and I've got you and you've got me. Do you know how much I love you Alanna?'

'As much as I love you,' she said. 'Now, take me to bed and hold me.'

They woke early, of course. Finn phoned the sister on the paediatric intensive care unit at once and held the receiver so that Alanna could hear the other side of the conversation.

'She's had a very good night, improved a lot,' said the sister. 'She's a strong little girl, and she'll be fine. Give us a couple of hours and then come down to see her. Mr Kershaw will be here then. I know he'll want a chat.'

'We'll see you then,' Finn said, and replaced the receiver.

Alanna lowered her head back onto the pillow. 'I would really have liked to go to see her now,' she said plaintively.

'You're a nurse, you know what it's like at handover. We'd only be in the way. Anyway, before we see Eleanor we really need to talk for a while. We know she's in good hands and we might not get this chance again. Now, there's a kettle on the table over there. Fancy a cup of tea?'

It all seemed strangely ordinary to Alanna but she realised that, yes, she was thirsty. So she watched as Finn climbed out of bed—dressed only in a pair of rather attractive dark blue boxer shorts—and made them both tea. He put her mug on the bedside table and leaned over to kiss her, longingly, lovingly on the lips. Then he climbed back into bed beside her.

'This isn't about Eleanor,' he said. 'In some ways it never has been about her. This is about you and me. Ever since you decided to come to Benthwaite, this has been about us two. Tell me, Alanna, what did you think about as you walked over the fell into the town? What were you looking for?'

'I thought I wanted closure,' she said. 'I wanted things settled between us.'

'There's a difference between closing and settling. You must have had memories of our lives there together as you walked. What were those memories? Happy—or angry?'

She had to be honest. 'I remembered that you were the first, perhaps the only man I'd ever loved. And that made me angry. Angry with myself, that is. But then I was angry with you when I saw you with a little girl and thought you had had a child…a child…' Her voice trailed away.

'Go on,' he asked gently.

'A child without me.'

He nodded. 'That's very understandable. Next question. Why did you agree to stay when Harry offered you the job for three months? Being close to me, after we had fought so hard, it should have been the last thing you wanted. And you didn't know about Eleanor then.'

'I don't know. It sounds silly. Perhaps I might have changed my mind and…'

He pressed her. 'Are you sure you don't know?'

She didn't answer. He stretched out his arm, ran a finger up her arm, from wrist to shoulder. She had no night clothes and, like him, had spent the night clad solely in her underwear. It was a delicate caress but she shivered with the excitement that it caused in her.

'Are you sure you don't know why you took the job?' His voice was still soft, still tempting.

She knew what he wanted her to say, and suddenly she knew that he was right. 'I wanted to see more of you,' she said. 'I wanted to be with you again, if only for a while. Perhaps after a while the anger I felt would have driven me away. But I couldn't just move out of your life after one meeting. I'd spent four years wandering the globe, looking for something. I didn't find it, largely because I didn't know what it was. Perhaps, it was just possible, I'd left it behind.'

She turned towards him, the bedclothes, bunched precariously over her shoulders, fell to her waist. She grabbed his hands, pulled them towards her, pressed them firmly against her breasts and held them there. 'Finn, you're pulling my soul out here! I'm telling you things I didn't know myself and it hurts. Now it's your turn. What did you feel, the first time you saw me again?'

Gently, he took his hands from her breasts, wrapped his arms around her and pulled her to him. She thought she could feel the beating of his heart against her. Or was it her own heart beating?

'Like you, I tried to fool myself. But when I saw you…there was a flash and I remembered what I had lost. And I felt so sad. But then…'

She nodded. 'We both kidded ourselves, didn't we? We didn't just hide our feelings from each other—we hid them from ourselves.'

'That's the way we were brought up.'

'We know that now. And since we know it, we won't do it again. We'll start by doing better with Eleanor. Finn, while I was away with Gabriel, I realised I don't want another three months or six weeks or even five minutes before I make up my mind about you or anything else. In fact, I don't want the last couple of weeks I'm entitled to. I love you. I know exactly what I want and there's no doubt and there'll be no going back.'

He kissed her then and she felt that never had

she been happier. He started, 'So will you—'
But she held up her finger to stop him.

'Before you go any further.' She reached over
to where her jeans had been thrown over a chair,
felt in the zipped-up back pocket and took out a
wallet. From the wallet she took a tiny packet
wrapped in tissue paper. 'You might want to
borrow this,' she said. 'I've been carrying it
around with me everywhere. In case it was
suddenly needed.'

He took the packet from her, threw away the
tissue paper and there was her wedding ring.

'Sweetheart, will you marry me—again—but
in church this time? You can wear the ring, teach
Eleanor to call you Mummy, be Mrs Cavendish
again. And soon, very soon, we can see about
getting Eleanor a baby brother or sister.'

'Of course I'll marry you, Finn. You'll make
me the happiest woman in the world. And I'll
make you happy, too. I'll be Eleanor's mummy
and as for a brother or sister for her?' Alanna
slid down the bed. 'We could always start trying
now…'

MEDICAL™

━━━━ᨀ━━━━ *Large Print* ━━━━ᨀ━━━━

Titles for the next six months...

August

THE DOCTOR'S BRIDE BY SUNRISE	Josie Metcalfe
FOUND: A FATHER FOR HER CHILD	Amy Andrews
A SINGLE DAD AT HEATHERMERE	Abigail Gordon
HER VERY SPECIAL BABY	Lucy Clark
THE HEART SURGEON'S SECRET SON	Janice Lynn
THE SHEIKH SURGEON'S PROPOSAL	Olivia Gates

September

THE SURGEON'S FATHERHOOD SURPRISE	Jennifer Taylor
THE ITALIAN SURGEON CLAIMS HIS BRIDE	Alison Roberts
DESERT DOCTOR, SECRET SHEIKH	Meredith Webber
A WEDDING IN WARRAGURRA	Fiona Lowe
THE FIREFIGHTER AND THE SINGLE MUM	Laura Iding
THE NURSE'S LITTLE MIRACLE	Molly Evans

October

THE DOCTOR'S ROYAL LOVE-CHILD	Kate Hardy
HIS ISLAND BRIDE	Marion Lennox
A CONSULTANT BEYOND COMPARE	Joanna Neil
THE SURGEON BOSS'S BRIDE	Melanie Milburne
A WIFE WORTH WAITING FOR	Maggie Kingsley
DESERT PRINCE, EXPECTANT MOTHER	Olivia Gates

™MILLS & BOON®
Pure reading pleasure™

0708 LP 2P P1 Medical

MEDICAL™

Large Print

November
NURSE BRIDE, BAYSIDE WEDDING   Gill Sanderson
BILLIONAIRE DOCTOR, ORDINARY   Carol Marinelli
NURSE
THE SHEIKH SURGEON'S BABY   Meredith Webber
THE OUTBACK DOCTOR'S SURPRISE BRIDE Amy Andrews
A WEDDING AT LIMESTONE COAST   Lucy Clark
THE DOCTOR'S MEANT-TO-BE MARRIAGE   Janice Lynn

December
SINGLE DAD SEEKS A WIFE   Melanie Milburne
HER FOUR-YEAR BABY SECRET   Alison Roberts
COUNTRY DOCTOR, SPRING BRIDE   Abigail Gordon
MARRYING THE RUNAWAY BRIDE   Jennifer Taylor
THE MIDWIFE'S BABY   Fiona McArthur
THE FATHERHOOD MIRACLE   Margaret Barker

January
VIRGIN MIDWIFE, PLAYBOY   Margaret McDonagh
DOCTOR
THE REBEL DOCTOR'S BRIDE   Sarah Morgan
THE SURGEON'S SECRET BABY WISH   Laura Iding
PROPOSING TO THE CHILDREN'S   Joanna Neil
DOCTOR
EMERGENCY: WIFE NEEDED   Emily Forbes
ITALIAN DOCTOR, FULL-TIME FATHER Dianne Drake

 MILLS & BOON®
Pure reading pleasure™   0708 LP 2P P2 Medical